MW01274844

Western Tide

The Outlaw

Sunset, summer of 1875. Wyoming. These were dangerous times, even for bandits, gunslingers, and desperados. The year before, Custer had led an expedition into the Black Hills looking for gold and got the Indians on the warpath. Then the U.S. government ordered all the Indians in Wyoming to report to reservations or face military action. The whole state was a powder keg ready to explode

A lone figure in a long, tattered leather duster down to his boots, with a collar that, when stuck up, rose to the top of his cowboy hat. The brim of his hat was down over his eyes to keep his face hidden from possible lawmen patrolling the town. As he rode into town the only thing that was visible was his long, long dark brown hair that went down to the middle of his back, and a thick beard and mustache.

His clothes were nothing special, neither. Chaps, boots with spurs, and a shirt that had seen better days. His duster was stained beyond cleaning with a combination of the trail and the saloon as was his cowboy hat with the front being mangled from some sort of fight.

The cowboy appeared to be desperate and in a big hurry. He had his hand on the top of his hat, keeping it on his head like he was a rodeo rider as he went from wanted poster to wanted poster.

He rode his horse low in the saddle trying to stay as unremarkable as possible invisible; trying to stay in the shadows of the town's main street stealing glances at his picture on the wanted posters. It wasn't hard for him to stay in the darkness since the sun was setting and all the awnings were providing plenty of shade.

He wasn't finding what he was looking for. What he was finding were a bunch of portraits of nasty-looking guys. There were a bunch of wanted posters that belonged to men that had threatening, ugly and snarling looks in their portraits. They were the worst of the worst.

The rider noticed that the rewards got bigger as he went down the list, and the crimes were more numerous and more heinous as he went along.

The man stopped dead in his tracks and almost tumbled over when he found the wanted poster he was looking for. It was the poster for his best friend: Derek Rhodes.

The wanted poster for Derek Rhodes was much different than all the others. For one thing, the bounty on him was the most highest. It was $50,000. And, he was wanted dead or alive. There was an extra note under that; the governor of Wyoming wanted Rhodes alive so he could tear him apart, but he also wanted him dead because the sight of his corpse would bring him enough joy die a happy man. It was signed by Wyoming's senior sheriff, who also really hated Derek.

Another thing that was unique to Derek's wanted poster was his face. He was the only face on the row of wanted posters that didn't have a snarl or ugly look. No, Derek had a broad, happy, slightly open-mouthed smile with two rows of shiny white teeth. On top of that, Derek was one of the only handsome, clean faces on the posters. He was clean-shaven, had slick, combed-back black hair with curls in the back and went down to the bottom of his neck. Much shorter hair than his best friend. And, sure enough, his friend noticed that the sketch-guy had gotten Derek's brown eyes that all the girls talked about. The only thing about Derek that wasn't right was a crescent-moon shaped scar on his right cheek. Derek never told anyone how he got it, and nobody knew.

Derek's friend ripped the wanted poster off the wall and rode hard out of town. It was one of the most populous towns in Wyoming that he'd ridden through. The streets and alleyways were pretty much in darkness, but every single window in every room and building there, even the church, was bright with lights and booming with noise and activity. He could see people drinking and partying through every window.

The cowboy carefully put the wanted poster inside his jacket and took out a clean sheet of paper and a writing utensil. He began to carefully map-out the town with a lot of attention to detail. He did a lot of erasing and redrawing. He wanted the drawing to be perfect. His main focus was making sure that he had the correct placement of the town's local bank. But, he took his time to put in landmarks in the town that weren't significant. For example, he drew the church that was way at the end of the main street and not connected to anything else in the town.

Once the map was finished, the cowboy carefully put that in his pocket and then ran toward the stables. He leapt clean over the surrounding fence and landed perfectly on his horse.

"That sort of move looks familiar," the kid working at the stables commented. "I can't quite remember who does that."

"Yeah, I just did it," the cowboy said, flipping the kid a coin.

The cowboy didn't want to tip the kid off that he just performed a move that was the trademark of his best friend and boss, Derek Rhodes. People knew Derek for his acrobatics getting on his horse. It didn't matter to him how high the jump was, how far, or what he jumped over. He would get to his horse in the most dangerous and creative way he could, trying his hardest to dazzle people as he did it. He never failed.

"Wait," the kid said as the cowboy started to kick his horse into attention.

"Aren't you…"

"No!" the cowboy yelled, as his horse jumped over the fence and into the forest.

The cowboy also didn't want the kid to find out that he was Tom Johnson, the best friend of Wyoming's most wanted outlaw, Derek Rhodes. That would have blown the lid off their entire scheme.

Tom had also taken the time to track the quickest path from the town to his gang's camp. That didn't ease his mind, though. Every little noise or shadow he saw made him even more nervous. He was constantly looking over his shoulder and keeping his head on a swivel. Everything startled him: owl hoots, chipmunk squeaks, twigs breaking and any shadows that he thought he saw. During the entire ride, he kept reaching into his jacket to make sure that he still had the map he drew and the wanted poster.

Tom's horse slowed down to a trot when he came into a clearing where the gang was holed up. The outlaw gang of Derek Rhodes.

There was a huge bonfire in the center of the clearing with flames that almost reached the top of the rocky outcrop. That meant that the smoke could probably be seen. Tom did not like that; he didn't like the idea that the gang was knowingly, or unknowingly, possibly giving away their position. However, it was almost impossible for Tom to ever be totally at peace. His mind was always in a state of unease. That's just how he was.

Tom found Derek in a card game on the ground with some of the oldest gang members, save for Tom. There was the slave they freed, Otis, the big, fat, jolly bar-brawler from Texarcana, Tex, and a Mexican runaway, Villegas. Of course, there was Derek.

Tom would have known Derek was there without even looking. Derek liked to hear himself talk, and to have everyone else hear him talk. There was only one person boisterous enough to attempt to match him at yapping, and that was Tex. But, he could never go toe-to-toe with Derek.

"Hey, Tom Johnson!" Derek yelled, looking up. "Come on down and watch me milk these guys of the very pants they're wearing!"

Derek was also the flashiest one in the bunch. He had himself a nice, clean, fresh black leather jacket that fit him just right. He also had himself a pair of fine rattlesnake-skin cowboy boots, and a sly, black cowboy hat with a slightly ovular-shaped brim and the sides slightly curved upward, but not too much. Derek was careful about the way his hat looked because he was very particular about that kind of thing.

There was an immediate backlash at Derek's comment.

"You've been betting on manure all night, I'm going to raise the stakes," Villegas said, tossing a few dollars into the pot.

"Me, too," Tex said, matching Villegas' bet.

"What do you say, Otis?" Derek asked, elbowing Otis.

"I want to see you go down once," Otis said, putting his share in. "So, I'm in."

They all exchanged their cards to Tex, the dealer, who dealt them the new portions of their hands.

"All in," Derek said with a serious face.

"Aw, hell," Tex said, throwing his cards in.

"Yeah, phooey," Otis said, tossing his cards in.

"What do you say, Villegas?" Derek asked.

"I call you," Villegas said, going all in.

"Have I been betting on manure all night, amigo?" Derek asked, grinning.

"Uh-oh!" Tex yelled, bellowing.

"Take a gander," Derek said, revealing his cards to Villegas. He had a full house.

"I quit," Villegas said, tossing his pair of sevens and junk into the pile.

"There we go," Derek said, collecting his winnings. "This is for all of you. Thanks for playing."

Derek flipped a coin to each man, who let it fall on the ground.

"The money's just gonna sit there, fellas," Derek said as they all walked away.

"Could we have a word, Derek?" Tom asked.

"Oh, a word from Tom Johnson," Derek said, picking up a bottle of beer and taking a swig. "I feel like I'm in big trouble."

"No-" Tom said, cringing. "Do you want to be hung-over for the heist tomorrow?"

"Tom," Derek said, slapping Tom's shoulder, "I'll just get drunk when I get up in the morning and totally pass-over that hangover, brother."

"Yeah, prolong disaster," Tom said. "That way, you'll be a complete wreck when sheriff Hatcher rides in with an army of deputies that have been indoctrinated to hate you and all of us."

"You really think the worst of everything, don't you?" Derek asked, finding his friends neurosis funny, as he always did.

Derek and Tom couldn't have had more different personalities as best friends. Derek was a free spirit that never let anything bother him. Derek lived his life carefree. Then, there was uptight Tom who was always nervous about everything, always worried and always nit-picking. Tom could never settle down. He was always tightly wound-up.

"I do my best to make sure everything that we do goes right," Tom said. "And it bothers me that our entire plan could be blown because of stupid mistakes and that you seemingly don't care."

"Tommy," Derek said, starting to get a little drunk, "how many times have we pulled through off a job and made it out? Nobody can touch us!"

"Oh, that kind of attitude is just not right," Tom said, rubbing his forehead.

"Tom, you have to relax," Derek said. "Here, have some of this."

Derek offered Tom his beer. Tom slapped it out of his hand.

"I swear to God," Tom said to Derek, "I'm not going to have us all get caught because you were drunk. Can we get down to business, please?"

"Yes, let's get down to business," Derek said.

"Very good," Tom said, pulling the map out. "I made an accurate rendering of the town with an approximate scale that you can reference down here in the corner."

Derek almost fell over while he was laughing. Tom was looking very serious and impatient.

"I really don't see what's funny," Tom snapped.

"You made a distance scale!" Derek said, trying to slow his laughing down. "So, that's where you were."

"Yeah, that's where I was," Tom said. "I was at the town, working on the plan while you guys were here gambling and partying. I was on top of things, as always."

"That's why we have you around," Derek said. "We let Tom worry about everything so we don't have to."

"It's a good thing, too," Tom said. "On account of I'm the only that can do this thing properly. Now, take a look. The bank is right here. I couldn't find any sheriff stations in town. I figure that means Hatcher has a big outpost close to here."

"I wouldn't worry about Hatcher," Derek said to Tom. "If that big lug hasn't caught us by now, he never will."

"Well, he can't just worry about us," Tom argued. "He's got Bolton Butler's gang, and the whole state."

"No, he's been following us since the east border," Derek said, chuckling. "And we've given him the slip every time. What, what's the problem?"

Tom was rubbing his forehead again.

"Derek," Tom said, breathing heavily, "you didn't think to warn us that the sheriff of Wyoming was trailing us? A sheriff that's wanted to put us behind bars for years under orders from a governor that's wanted to hang us since the beginning of his term? Was that not all that important, Derek?"

"See, that's why I didn't tell you," Derek said. "I knew you'd get all worked-up over it and lose your nerve."

"No, hold it," Tom said, about to rebuttal. "No, that's probably true.

"I thought you noticed all those deputies we've been running into."

"I didn't think anything of it," Tom said. "Could I show you something?"

Tom pulled the wanted poster out of his jacket.

"That's a fine-looking wanted poster," Derek said, taking it. "They got my good side."

"Oh, really?" Tom asked, even more frustrated that Derek didn't care he was on a wanted poster. "Which side is your good side?"

"Both of 'em," Derek said, handing Tom the wanted poster back and laughing.

"This is not funny," Tom said. "You're wanted for half a million for a whole list of crimes, and it's only the stuff they know about. Look at the little note under 'dead or alive'."

Derek read the note and laughed.

"Yeah, I bet," Derek said.

"When you act this under these kinds of circumstances, it keeps me awake at night," Tom said. "It makes me start to prepare myself to go to prison the next day, Derek!"

"I tell you what," Derek said to Tom, "I'll play everybody a song."

"That's not… gonna help," Tom said as Derek walked over to a log with a guitar propped-up on it.

It was a guitar that Derek made himself. He was something of a musician. He could play guitar, sing and play piano. He could pick up any instrument and start playing it and playing it well. His favorite was the guitar. He made it himself. He was also something of a handyman and artisan. He put a polished finish on the body of the guitar that gave it a perpetual shine.

"My hat, please," Derek said as everyone started to make a crowd in front of him.

A short, skinny kid with short, orange hair tossed Derek his hat. Derek caught it and put it on his head.

"Thanks, Marcus," Derek said to the kid.

Derek sat back and started playing. He was playing a new song that he had just thought of. It was a really fast tune with a happy and soothing melody. Derek was good at mixing different sounds into one song.

The entire gang was mystified by Derek's playing. They all sat on their hands with their eyes wide and with dumb smiles as they listened to Derek. His music had an even bigger effect on girls.

Tom was the only who wasn't effected by Derek's music. He was busy pacing around the campsite, picking up empty beer bottles and scrap, the whole time muttering about the pig-sty that the gang made at the campsite. He also didn't like that Derek was wailing on the guitar as loud as he could. He was nervous that the sheriff might hear it. But, Tom was just happy that Derek wasn't singing. That would have been the giveaway that Sheriff Ralph Hatcher needed to find them.

Derek was a very good gang leader. The guys all idolized him, looked up to him, and trusted him with their lives. Nobody in the gang ever questioned him, except for Tom. But, that was generally accepted and okay with Derek. Derek and Tom were such close friends that Tom got a slide for pestering Derek and everybody else all the time.

Derek tried to keep the gang close together like a family. He learned that was a much more effective system of organization than to just rope a bunch of nasty criminals together and let them do what they do. He and Tom got to experience that with their first gang, whose leader is now their rival, Bolton Butler.

The gang had gotten pretty numerous over the years; Derek had close to thirty men in his ranks by then, and he tried his best to stay personal with everybody. But, he couldn't handle much more than his original men: Tom, Tex, Villegas and Otis. Derek kept an eye on sixteen-year-old Marcus who needed some looking-out for.

Derek was a pretty unique guy, but anyone would say that Tex was the closest thing to another Derek Rhodes, and it was only by way of personality. Tex was the biggest guy in the bunch in every sense of being big. He was a full head taller than Tom, who was tall to begin with. Tex was about as wide as two men standing side by side, and as fat. He had a big, wide, chubby face topped with a huge bush of brown, curly hair. He had legs and arms like tree trunks. He knew how to use his weight to his advantage. He was easy to see, and he was easy to hear. He was extremely loud, Tom would say even a little obnoxious. He had a signature boisterous laugh that could echo at any location.

Villegas had been a Mexican national up until he had enough and migrated to America. He had some gold and silver teeth and an unusually long tongue. He had shoulder-long curly hair that was a mixture of white and black streaks. Of course, he had really tan skin.

Otis was released from his plantation a few years after the Civil War by Derek and Tom. He was actually the oldest guy in the gang. His skin as really, really dark skin and he had short, curly, gray/black hair.

Marcus was the real handyman in the gang. The gang found him making carts and saddles for a sheriff's department in South Wyoming. Derek and the gang got him out of there because he was an orphan and the sheriff and his deputies weren't treating him well.

There was one guy, like Marcus, that was on the outside looking into Derek's inner circle. That was the man they called Surge. That was short for surgeon, because he used to be a doctor. He left the profession and joined Derek's gang when he wasn't getting any patients because the governor was forcing doctors to charge ridiculous fees to keep up with the high taxes. Surge was one of the only real intellectuals in the group. Tom seemed smart to people like Tex, but he was just a worrier. He wasn't really that bright. Surge, though, was. He looked it, too. He always had a pair of glasses that made his eyes look a little big. He had a big, hooked nose and really thin cheeks. He just jumped right into the whole outlaw lifestyle; he wasn't a fit individual.

The governor of Wyoming's hound dog was let off his leash and on the loose. True to what Derek "warned" Tom, senior Sheriff of Wyoming Ralph Hatcher was doggedly trying to capture Derek and his gang. He was so determined and hell-bent on getting Derek, that he had gone through waves and waves of young deputies that Derek and his gang had easily slaughtered. But, that didn't mean anything to Ralph. His deputies were just pawns.

Ralph's appearance was as ugly as his black heart. His skin was very leathery, wrinkly and dry. His brown hair was even longer than Tom's, and it was very stiff, dirty and in dreadlocks. He did have a thick beard that was soaked in dirt and mud all the time. His teeth, that were only visible when he was snarling, were puke-green and rotting. Villegas always made jokes about how his teeth were much better than the sheriff's. He was about as tall as Tom, too, and he had really long, bony fingers with nails that looked like talons.

Ralph Hatcher, more than anyone, believed in strength in numbers. That was very different from Derek, who was something of a lone-wolf with a lot of friends. Ralph was always surrounded by multiple, armored deputies. People associated the sheriff with a big mob that they had to deal with, and that effectively scared a lot of people into submission. On top of that, the governor always gave the sheriff extremely loose oversight on conduct, and the sheriff had nearly total discretion to him and his deputies.

Ralph and his men were in the town that Derek and his gang had most recently passed through. They did exactly what they did at every town; they held-up the local bank and took the state and federal government's money for themselves. Tom, even though nobody in the gang really cared, calculated that they usually took in the same amount of money than they would have if they cleaned the private accounts.

The sheriff and his new batch of deputies were met as they strolled into town by a bunch of kids who worked at the stables.

"The procedure may be a little different for us than you're used to," Ralph barked at the kids in his scratchy voice. "Ya'll put these horses in clean spots in those stables. These are government horses; they're worth more than you."

Ralph spat a disgusting loogie on the ground and looked at his new deputies. They all looked like regular guys that didn't really have much of a shot against Derek and his men. But, Ralph didn't see that. Ralph was going to do anything to get Derek.

"Alright, fellurs," Ralph said to them, "I don't know how much you really know about tax collecting, but the way we do it in Wyoming is we just show people the badge and beat the money out of 'em if they don't give it up first. Got it?"

They all nodded.

"Then, let's get to collecting."

The deputies started walking into buildings and taking money right out of people's pockets. Nobody fought back because they knew they were with Ralph, and didn't want to provoke him.

Ralph went straight for the town's local bank. He knew Derek's strategy of looting the state and federal government's money. Luckily for Ralph, this town was relatively friendly to the governor and the Sheriff.

Ralph entered the bank to find that it was in a normal condition. The gang hadn't destroyed it like they sometimes did.

"Rhodes and his boys come through here?" Ralph asked the clerk.

"Sure did, Sheriff," the clerk said. "Took everything that belonged to the governor and DC."

Ralph took his hat off and spat on the floor.

"Not to worry," Ralph said. "I'm on his tail and we're going to bring him on soon. We're one step ahead of him on this one. Based on the direction he's taking, I have deputies standing as bank clerks at the next bank en route. Gonna ambush him."

"Good thinking," the clerk said.

This was not Ralph's idea. He was dumber than a tree stump. The governor was the one who did all the plotting.

"Stay citizen-like, you hear?" Ralph asked the clerk.

"Yes, sir," the clerk said.

Ralph walked out of the bank and into the town's local pub. He was proud to find his rookie deputies taking everything; they were emptying the bar tender's tip jar, the band's tip jar, the safe, the register, and everyone's pockets. That's how they did things in Wyoming.

Ralph sat down at the counter. The bar tender didn't look happy to see him.

"Let me have a whiskey," Ralph said, putting his feet up on the countertop.

"Don't worry yourself about the tip," the bar tender said, pouring Ralph his glass. "I don't expect much."

"Ya'll shouldn't," Ralph said. "And, do I detect a tone?"

"I sure hope so," the bar tender said, slamming the shot glass on the countertop. "Listen, I'm all for law enforcement and public servants, but this reign of terror thing is wearing thin."

"Well, that's just too damn bad," Ralph said. "Because there ain't nothing you pathetic little people can do to us."

"You may want to rethink your meaning of the word 'little people' because I've got some guys who are gonna rock your world," the bar tender threatened. "Would you care to close my bar for me?"

Ralph took out his revolver and shot off two rounds in the ceiling. That caused a ruckus.

"Ya'll scram, now!" Ralph ordered. "Go on, git!"

Everyone ran out of the bar except for Ralph's deputies and an even-up amount of enormous thugs that worked at the bar.

Ralph noticed that the bar tender may have been reaching for a gun under the countertop. Knowing bar tenders, Ralph assumed it was a maximum-spreading shotgun.

"I would take my hand off the double-barrel if I were you," Ralph said, swigging his whiskey.

"We'll see," the bar tender said. "Fellas, the sheriff didn't pay for his drink. Let's not let him get away with that."

One of the big thugs shut the door of the bar and locked it.

"Let 'em, have it, boys," Ralph said to his deputies.

They immediately started a huge brawl. Ralph and the bar tender both stayed like statues where they were as bottles, chairs, sawdust, blood, teeth and bodies went flying every which way. The bar tender still had his hand on something and he was staring at Ralph with a really cross look.

The fight really did a number on the bar. The piano and all the instruments were completely dismantled, all the windows were smashed, and the floor was covered with bits of broken tables, chairs, glass, teeth and blood. At the end of the fight, the floor was also covered with the unconscious bodies of the bar tender's thugs.

"I'm gonna give you one more chance to get your damn hand off the gun," Ralph said, "before you wish you did."

The bar tender tried to be swift and bring the gun out all in one fluid motion and shove it into Ralph's face. Ralph grabbed the top of the barrel and brought the body of the barrel into the bar tender's face. The bar tender flew into a rack of bottles and was knocked out.

"I like this here gun," Ralph said, checking out the double-barrel shotgun. "Fellas, grab whatever you want. In the morning, we're after Derek Rhodes."

The next morning, Tom was in his usual panic. The sun was rising, and nobody was awake yet, just him. Tom was going around, angrily kicking and shaking people awake. People weren't happy with Tom.

Tom wanted to get to the town as quick as they could to avoid the sheriff and get out of there. The fact that everyone was sleeping in was damaging to his plan.

Tom had just kicked Otis awake.

"Tom, you're like my old slave owner!" Otis shouted.

"You're like a kid!" Tom shouted back. "No offense, Marcus." Marcus was still too tired to hear him.

Tom went over to Derek last. That really pissed him off. He didn't like that the leader of the group was the last one to wake up. Tom knelt down next to Derek and raised an open hand to smack him awake. Tom was about to swing, but held his hand back when he saw Derek's lips curl into a smile.

"You don't want to lose that hand, do ya?" Derek asked. He opened his eyes and looked at Tom.

"Derek, we've got a job to do," Tom said, "and I'll be damned if it's going to be shot because all of you loafs slept in."

"If I know the sheriff," Derek said, "and I do, he'll be lagging behind us because he's got a big, fat ass dragging behind him. Did you get any sleep last night?"

"A little," Tom said. "I felt we needed a lookout, and Tex's snoring kept me up most of the time. Could we get to business now?"

"Yeah, sure," Derek said.

Derek got up and jumped on his horse after he shot his two six-shooters for ammo. Everyone else was mounted and looking at him.

"What are we waiting for" Derek asked, beaming at everybody. He always got exited for their next job.

"I don't know," Tex said. "You."

"Well, I'm going," Derek said, rearing his horse, and then taking off into the forest.

Everyone kicked their horses into a gallop and followed Derek. Tom caught up to Derek on the way.

"Now, Derek, I also calculated the quickest way through the forest," Tom said, "so we can make a quick getaway. If we make a left right up here…"

"Tom, nothing personal," Derek said, "but I'm just not in the mood for that junk."

Derek's horse picked up speed and left Tom in the dust. The gang caught up with Derek and they all slowed down when they got into the town.

"I like this place," Derek said, hopping off his horse. "I could stay here for a while. Lay low, know what I'm saying, fellas?"

They all chuckled, but Tom was rebutting.

"No, no, no," Tom said, following Derek toward the bank. "We're in and out."

When they walked into the bank, Derek shoved his hands into the back of his jacket and got a grip on his guns. Everyone else had their guns out, but not pointed at anyone in the bank.

The clerks at the bank didn't react as most people did when they held-up banks.

"The governor wants to do some budget-cutting," Derek boasted to the room. "They're going to hand their money over to the regular folk."

"Really?" the clerk asked. "Ralph Hatcher said you'd say that."

The other clerks in the bank tried to draw their guns as quick as they could, but the gang was quick to get the jump on them. Before the fake clerks knew it, they were disarmed and shoved to the ground or into the walls.

"Hatcher had stand-ins," Tom said, laughing. "I would have never have guessed."

"I think he's too stupid to think of something that clever," Derek bellowed. "What do you think, Villegas?"

"Pienso que el hombre no tenga intelligencia," Villegas agreed.

"I know what he said," the head clerk told Derek.

"Ah," Derek said. "What'd he say?"

"He said to kill the governor," the clerk said.

The clerk tried to pull his shotgun out, but Derek whipped his two revolvers out and put a bullet from each gun into the deputy's chest. The deputy flew into the wall behind him and his corpse hit the floor face-down.

"Okay, fellas," Derek said, hopping over the counter and taking the key off the deputy's belt.

"Tom, help me loot Roth's safe," Derek said.

"Sure," Tom said, walking away from the deputy he was detaining. The deputy immediately tried to attack Tom, but Surge took a gun out and shot the deputy through the back of the head.

"Good shooting, Surge," Derek said. "Fellas, tie these guys up."

"What are we gonna do with 'em?" Otis asked.

"Leave 'em in a cow pasture," Tom suggested. "Maybe right next to a few cow pies."

All the outlaws laughed and started to hog-tie the deputies. Derek and Tom opened up the governor's bank vault, it was made of gold, and started to stuff all the gold bars and cash into sacks. Once the other outlaws were finished tying-up the deputies, they started to help Derek and Tom round-up the money. Once they did, Derek had a better idea. They stuffed the deputies in the vault, tossed the keys inside and shut the vault.

"Good thinking, boss," Surge said to Derek as they brought the sacks of money out to the horses.

"It just came to me," Derek said. "I'm surprised I haven't thought of that before."

They all tied the sacks of money to their horses. They all assumed they were going to make a run for it, but Derek reached into a sack and pulled out a huge wad of bills.

"Derek," Tom said, nervously, "we have to get a jump on the sheriff."

Derek looked over at the nearest bar.

"Guys," Derek said, "I want to taste alcohol when it's the government paying. What do ya'll say?"

"Absolutely," Tex said, taking out a handful of bills for himself.

"I have a really... **really** bad feeling about this," Tom groaned, reluctantly getting off his horse and grabbing his own bank bills.

They all followed Derek into the bar and began a near twenty-four hour time span of nonstop partying, drinking, music, darts, sex, prostitutes and gambling. The gang all referred to that kind of day as the "Derek Rhodes Olympics." They usually preformed that big blow-out at the end of their periodic three-month crime sprees, but Derek just had to have a little extra fun.

Tom, of course, was the only one who hated these parties. He rarely ever drank, so he was always sober enough to notice how stupid they were acting and the crazy stuff they did. Tom strongly did not approve.

These "Olympics" were getting a little crazier than usual. Tex had almost gotten into some big drunken fights that Tom had to stop, but everyone else in the gang was encouraging the fights to happen. Tom had to scold Marcus for being drunk while he was playing darts. But, what he found Derek doing disturbed him the most.

At around the time the sun was setting, Tom tried to find Derek in the town to let him have it for the fiasco when they could have been making the escape.

He heard Derek's voice in the top room of a stripper-joint and he opened the door. He felt foolish for not starting his search there, knowing Derek.

When Tom opened the door, he found Derek doing a sex-sandwich dance in between two strippers. One of the girls was wearing his cowboy hat and the other girl was wearing his leather jacket. He had his shirt off and he was twirling it in the air. He was wearing one of the girl's stripper bras over his bare chest.

"SWEET JESUS!" Tom shouted as he saw this.

Derek looked over at Tom. He was completely drunk out of his mind.

"Hey, Tommy!" Derek shouted. He looked at a third stripper that was waiting for her turn.

"Number 3," Derek said to her, "now we can do that double-layer I was talking about. Tom, add some more meat to this sandwich!"

"Derek," Tom said, "I very well would never get involved in a sexual… whatever you call this with you no matter how many girls are in between us."

"Huh," Derek said. "I guess we're different that way."

"Could I have a word with you, Derek?" Tom asked.

"Sure," Derek said, resuming the sex dance. "I'm listening."

Tom walked over to Derek and dragged him out of the room by his ear. Tom shut the door and released Derek.

"Did you just drag me out of there by my ear?" Derek said. "It kind of hurts."

"I sure did," Tom said. "You're acting like a child, so I'll treat you like on."

"But I'm the leader," Derek whined. "It's not fair."

"For God's sake," Tom said. "My daughter is more mature than you are."

"No, no," Derek said. "I only act childish when I'm drunk."

"I guess you got me," Tom said, frustrated. "Derek, is that lipstick on your mouth?"

Tom noticed Derek had lipstick that was crooked to his mouth.

"Oh, yeah," Derek said. "That was um…. I don't remember her name! Imagine that!"

"You never remember their names," Tom said.

"She's a rascal, though," Derek said, slapping Tom on the shoulder.

"Derek," Tom said, removing Derek's hand, "don't you see what's going on here? The sheriff is after us and you got everybody drunk and partying! How is this a good thing? I can't figure it out!"

"Tom, I don't know what to tell you," Derek said. "But, I've got this.... Your family is definitely well-t-do and under control. Your daughter has a good upbringing, I think."

"Yeah, thanks," Tom said. "Especially for that little part about the flattery, I almost passed that by. Derek, this is not good, this behavior."

"I'm enjoying it a whole lot," Derek argued.

"I'm seeing nearly the exact same demeanor when you bailed on Jess," Tom said. "Does that ring a bell?"

"You're a real party-downer, Tom," Derek said. "I don't want to talk about this right now."

"You're gonna have to talk about it sometime, Derek," Tom said. "And when you do, I'll talk about it with you. Just do me one thing, wear men clothes. This look on you is freaking me out."

"I can't make any promises!" Derek said, grinning. "Excuse me."

Tom stepped aside and let Derek go back in his room.

"This is going to be really bad," Tom said, thinking about what would happen if the sheriff showed up soon, which he would. Even Ralph Hatcher could handle a gang of passed-out criminals.

The next morning, Tom wasn't going to waste any time. He sheriff could arrive at any minute, and he wanted to get as much of a head start as he could. It was extremely tough to wake up all the guys the way they were: totally hung-over.

Tom was frantically running from building to building, trying to get everyone awake and ready to make a getaway. They really weren't happy with him.

"You know, Tom," Surge said, waking up, "a good amount of sleep is usually a good prescription for anything."

"Surge!" Tom shouted. "Last night you were destroying your liver with alcohol! Why can't you follow your own advice or give it to the rest of the gang?"

"To be fair," Surge said, putting on his glasses, "if all my patients followed my advice a hundred percent, I'd be out business!"

While Tom was thinking of something to say, he whiffed a horrid smell coming from Surge.

"Oh my God," Tom said, almost keeling-over and waving the air in front of his nose. "Why'd you have to eat so much fried chicken?!"

"I don't know," Surge said. "Why's it so good?"

"The sheriff is going to smell this from a mile away. Where's Derek?"

"Top floor, still," Surge reported.

Tom ran up to the room where he found Derek the night before. Derek was still there, sprawled on the floor among multiple sleeping hookers and snoring through the walls.

Tom shook Derek and awake and started to slap his face.

"What the hell?" Derek asked, rolling over.

"We have to get riding right now," Tom said, quickly.

A gunshot snapped him and Derek to attention. They both went to a window and looked down onto the main street to see Sheriff Ralph Hatcher and his deputies riding into the town.

"Shit," Tom said, kicking the wall. "I have no plan. I'm drawing a blank."

"Relax, Tom," Derek said.

"We should not split up," Tom thought. "Absolutely not."

"I disagree!" Derek said, running out of the room.

"Derek!" Tom quietly shouted. "Derek! Damn it! I got to get the rest of the guys out of here."

Otis, Tex and Villegas were hiding in an alley, looking out at Sheriff Hatcher.

"What do we do?" Villegas asked. "We're stuck and drunk."

"I going up on the roof," Otis said, putting a few bullets in his rifle. "Do some target practice."

Otis went around back of the nearest shop and took the stairs to the roof. He propped his rifle up on the roof's railing. He looked across to the other rooftop and saw Marcus on the rooftop right across from him and Tom on the on the next one over, and Surge was on the one next to Tom. The rest of the gang was probably getting ready to pounce on the sheriff and his deputies.

Tom was gearing up to snipe Ralph right then and there, but all the deputies and Ralph turned to the entrance of the town. Derek was walking down the street right toward them.

"That damn buffoon," Tom muttered to himself.

"I knew we'd catch up with you," Ralph shouted, pointing at Derek. Derek had his hands shoved into the back of his jacket again.

"Where are the stand-ins?" a deputy asked, with his shotgun right at Derek.

"They're locked in Roth's vault," Derek said, laughing. "Probably pissing all over themselves."

"I'm glad you have a sense of humor," Ralph said. "It'll keep you together in my prison."

"I don't think Roth will let you keep me alive," Derek said.

"Let's see your hands!" a deputy nervously shouted. They had never actually been on duty with an outlaw before.

Derek pulled out his two six-shooters and had his hands stretched to the sides like he was on a cross.

"Drop them!" Ralph shouted. "And stay put!"

"Make me!" Derek yelled.

"Drop him!" Ralph shouted.

The deputies were rookies, and were a bit hesitant to shoot a living person, criminal or not. That was their fatal mistake. Two of Derek's men jumped out of the alleys on each side of him and killed two of the deputies. Before any of the other deputies could fire upon Derek, the men on the roof started to fire upon the group of deputies. Ralph aimed his big revolver at Derek. Derek shot a bullet from one o his guns right into the barrel of Ralph's gun. Ralph's gun jammed and he dropped it.

A big cross-fire started between the deputies and the gang. The deputies spread out through the town. Ralph looked at Derek again. Derek shot his hat right off of his head.

Ralph lost Derek in the firefight. The truth was, all he really cared about was getting Derek. He didn't care about the rest of the gang, except that Tom always pointed out the legal obstructions the sheriff always committed. It was like a game between Ralph and Derek. Ralph was never looking to really kill Derek, just to "win." He really desired to throw Derek in jail. Derek always had great fun giving Ralph the slip each and every encounter they had. The real hatred was between Derek and Ralph's boss, the governor of Wyoming.

Ralph kept seeing flashes of Derek make his way toward the church at the end of the main street. He was positive he saw Derek run in through the front doors, and Derek did.

Ralph ran toward the church, trying to avoid gunshots. And there were plenty of gunshots. Derek and his gang were a double-edged sword. They were a slick-enough bunch to be able to get into places and get out with thousands of dollars, but they were also dangerous enough to completely destroy a town if they wanted to. They were all great marksmen who liked to see explosions and things of that nature.

Ralph's rookie deputies were not prepared at all for who they were up against. The ones that weren't dropped already were cowering wherever they could.

Tom didn't want to massacre kids, and that's who these deputies were. Once he realized that they had the deputies completely pinned-down, he ran into the middle of the street and called the firing off. What they did then was scare the deputies running off. They weren't going to report for duty with Ralph ever again. Derek and his gang could do that to people, too.

When Ralph got to the church, he took out another gun and slowly opened the door. He found the church to be completely empty. Even the priest had run away.

Ralph went over to the poor box and ripped the top off. Before he stuck his hand in and took the money for himself, a big bowie knife flew by and knocked the gun out of his hand and sawed through the barrel.

Ralph looked up and saw Derek dash behind the altar and out of sight. Ralph ran over behind the altar and couldn't find Derek. He ran back out into the church and saw a tail-end of rope go up the staircase that was right next to the poor box. Ralph ran over there and noticed that the knife wasn't by his busted gun anymore.

Ralph ran up the stairs and got to the roof. Derek was standing there with the rope tied around his waist.

"Why don't you fight me, chicken shit?" Ralph asked.

"Would a chicken shit do this, sheriff?" Derek asked.

Derek got a running start and swan-dived off the roof. Ralph ran to the side where Derek jumped off and saw him suspended with the tightened rope, right over his horse. The rest of the gang was on their horses and ready to ride. They all had their sacks of money from the bank tied to their horses.

Derek used his bowie knife to cut through the rope and he landed on his horse.

"Maybe next time, Sheriff!" Derek shouted at Ralph as he and his gang rode away.

"That was a pretty good one, actually!" Ralph yelled back. He spat off the roof of the church. Derek had given him the slip again.

Working Family

Every morning before the sun was even up, Rodney McGillis was always woken up in the middle of his sleep by his father, Stanley McGillis. Rod was so used to this ritual and so averse to keeping his father waiting that he always woke himself up a little earlier so he could get right up out of bed and ready to get to work outside.

Stanley was a very salty and grizzled person. He was a Union soldier in the Civil War and fought in the uncivilized territories. So, he was used to pretty tough conditions and that made him mean and rugged. His leg was rendered useless after it was hit by a Confederate cannon ball and broke it multiple times. He wouldn't amputate, though. He went around for the rest of his days with a crutch and a crooked leg.

Stanley scared a lot of people, despite his slight immobility. His bad leg didn't do much to slow down his grit; he was a very strong guy and was still good at fighting. But, underneath his short, curly, black hair, behind his thick, black beard and in between his thick, black sideburns there was a thick-skinned face with very dark, angry eyes accompanied by a very stern expression. Stanley was very, very serious. Rod had never seen him smile in his entire life.

Rod was much different from his father. Rod was a very striking sixteen-year-old. He had light brown hair that was close to reaching his shoulders. His mother and sister encouraged him to keep his hair parted in the front so the "girls could see his handsome face." He did that as much as he could, but cared a lot more about helping his father maintain the family farm. Rod was fit enough to do his own share and take over his father's work, anyway. He was pretty tall, very lean, and he had a lot of natural strength. Rod had been doing real work on the farm his entire life and it did a lot of good for him.

Stanley limped into his son and daughter's room and found Rod to already be sitting up in his bed and getting his boots on.

"You're up already?" Stanley asked Rod in his gruff, slightly Scottish voice.

"You bet, pa," Rod said, standing up.

"Well," Stanley said, turning himself to walk out of the kids' room, "I'll meet you downstairs."

Stanley's thumping on the floor with his crutch woke up his nine-year-old daughter.

"It doesn't look like morning yet," she said, sitting up and looking out the window.

She was right; the sky was still black and the only light that was in their room was a little lantern that Stanley had in his free hand.

"No, honey," Stanley said, this time in as soft a tone as he could. "Go back to sleep."

"Lucky you," Rod said, walking over to her and giving her a kiss.

"Mama and I are gonna have a big meal for you and papa when you get back in," his sister promised him.

"Molly, your breakfasts are the only reason I like getting up in the morning," Rod said to his sister.

"Rod," Stanley barked, "we're wasting time."

"Go get 'em today," Molly said, slapping Rod's arm and going back to sleep.

Rod left the room and walked downstairs with his father.

"Go put those new parts in the rifle before we go," Stanley ordered.

"I took care of it last night," Rod said. "Before I went to bed I put the rifle back together."

"Good thinking," Stanley muttered, walking out the front door.

Rod ran into the barn and got his hunting rifle that was now furnished with brand new parts. He strapped it to his back and began his usual routine of maintaining the farm.

Rod was terrific at milking the cows. Right when his father began to teach him how to do it, Rod worked his tail off to have perfect technique and to be able to do it as quick as he can. Rod eventually got much better at milking cows than his father, but even that wouldn't impress Stanley. At this point, the only way another man could impress Stanley was to lose have his leg totally blown off.

Stanley walked into the barn while Rod was milking the cows and checked the rifle to make sure Rod really put the gun back together with new parts. He did.

Once Rod was done milking the cows, he took all the buckets of milk and ran them back to the front door of the farm for his mother and sister to pick up.

Next, Rod brought all the horses and cows into the ranch so they could graze and ride. Once he did that, Rod fed all the chickens. That was one part of his duties that he didn't like so much.

Once Rod had spread all the chicken feed around the floor of the coop, the sun was just about rising.

"Rod, we don't have all day," Stanley barked at him. "Let's get going."

Stanley and Rod weren't just farmers. They were also outdoorsmen. Rod and Stanley were big hunters, especially Stanley. In the war, he grew accustomed to being treated like a beast by other humans, so he naturally came to think of most other things as rodents that he could kill without remorse. He also didn't like Indians either because they supported the Confederates in the territories.

Even though Stanley innately loved to hunt, for sport, too, he always seemed to hate it because he always complained at how easy it was to kill the animals when he was so skilled at killing people. Not only that, Stanley had a huge body count of people that were trained to turn around and kill him.

Before they started hunting, the guys checked their fishing net that Rod had set-up just at the bending of a small river that they knew about. It was a good spot to put the net because the fish would get surprised by the net, which just appeared at the curvature of the river and they'd be trapped. Stanley learned that one when the hunting was bad at his camp during the war.

They got a quarter-full net's worth of fish. That was not good. Overnight, they used to be able to get themselves a full-net's worth of fish.

"That's weird," Rod said, dropping the net on the ground. "What do you figure's happening?"

Stanley looked down the river. He saw that there was a heap of waste flowing toward the net.

"Don't drop it back in, Rod," Stanley warned. "Leave it here."

Rod dropped the net on the ground. He didn't know why they weren't catching a lot of fish, but Stanley did. He knew it was because the governor was allowing railroad owners to dump waste into the rivers and lakes, and that was killing the fish. But, Stanley hated making excuses and complaining.

They never had any trouble hunting. Stanley and Rod knew the territory in their "backyard" almost just as well as the animals that lived there. They knew all the caves, dens, mountains and valleys. Even though they loved hunting, they knew how to respect the wilderness.

And they really loved the patch of earth they were living on. The forests were thick, green, dense, healthy and full of wonder. The mountains were high and mighty, and the valleys exentuated the height of the mountains.

Rod was a good shot. He could hit anything that he could see from the top of any of the mountains. Stanley was much better, though, but he wanted Rod to do as much work as he could make him do on the farm.

Stanley was very, very tough on Rod. He treated all men he interacted with like the guys in his unit during the war treated each other. The reason for that was because he wanted Rod to be able to take care of himself, a farm and a family all by himself. Rod knew this and appreciated Stanley very much. Either way, Rod was a sportsman and hard-worker at heart. He was glad to have a father to push him as much as Stanley did.

And Stanley didn't let his injury slow him down. He could make it up any slope just behind Rod's pace and didn't need any help. He was too proud to have anyone help him with his disability.

It was a good hunting day. Rod cleanly brought down a full-grown buck. On the way back to the farm at around noon time, Rod and Stanley lugged the buck's body back together and Rod dragged the fish net back. They checked their traps on the way, but they hadn't gotten anything.

When they got back to their farm, now not in the shade of the dreary morning that only Stanley liked, they were greeted by a huge golden retriever. The apparently smiling dog ran right up to Rod, got on its hind legs and slapped his tongue all over his face. Rod didn't mind, but Stanley did.

"Get the hell down," Stanley said, slapping the dog. The dog whimpered and got down on all fours.

"Rod, you can make it to the barn with this beast, can't you?" Rod asked, dropping the back leg of the buck.

"Of course I can," Rod said, dragging the buck's body over to the barn.

Stanley dragged the net of fish to the house. He was met on the front porch by Molly while Rod dragged the buck's body into the barn and left it there. Molly ran in to see the big buck.

"Wow, that's huge!" she exclaimed, looking at it.

"Well, maybe to you," Rod joked. Molly smacked his arm.

Molly was very short, even for a nine-year-old, and especially when she was next to anyone in her family. Everyone whose last name was McGillis except Molly was pretty tall.

Molly was definitely daddy's girl. Stanley was very old-fashioned believing that the son should be toughened-up and worked, but not the daughter. Rod was never jealous about that. Even as her brother Rod babied her.

Molly had long, straight, shiny, black hair, her father's black hair. She had big, light blue eyes and pale skin as a result of not being out in the sun that much, like Rod and Stanley were.

"What happened to the rest of the fish?" Molly asked. "Papa's net looked a little empty."

"I guess those fish are getting wise to where we place the net," Rod said.

The big golden retriever ran into the barn and up to Rod. Rod patted his chest to encourage the dog to jump up again, which he did, and Rod let the dog lick his face some more. The McGillis', except Stanley, were big dog people. Stanley only liked to hunt animals, not live with them. But, Molly asked for it, so he caved.

"Couldn't you ask papa not to hit Sunny?" Molly asked Rod.

"Could **you** ask him?" Rod asked. "He wouldn't hit you."

"Probably not," Molly said.

"Oh my goodness," Mrs. McGillis, Sally, remarked, walking in the barn and looking at the big buck.

"That's the biggest one you've ever bagged, Rod."

"Yeah," Rod said. "I shot him in the face so we could eat him without any problems. Where's pa?"

"He walked right into our room and fell asleep," Sally said. "So, that's more food for you."

Rod, Sally, Molly and Sunny all walked into the main house of the farm and they all sat down at the kitchen table. Since Stanley wasn't there, Sunny sat in his seat. That would have been blasphemy if Stanley were actually there, but everyone else was fine with it.

"Rod, I made this flapjack special for you," Molly said, forking a plate off a short stack and putting it on his plate.

"Chocolate chips?" Rod asked, looking at it. "How did you get that idea? Because you're sweet?"

Molly and Sally laughed. The McGillis' were a very close family. Rod did have a best friend that was a guy and his age, but he also had his sister and mother. Because Stanley never let Molly go into town when Rod did, she only had Rod to spend time with at the farm, and she looked up to him.

Rod and Sally had a dynamic like Stanley and Molly. Sally appreciated that Rod did pretty much all the work in the house, and was always ready to let him off the hook with Molly.

Stanley made an entrance into the kitchen. The first thing he noticed was Sunny sitting in his chair.

"Get the hell out of my chair," Stanley snapped, shoving the dog out of the chair. Sunny went right over to Molly; she always handed him extra food that she couldn't finish.

"Rod, what kind of flapjack are you eating?" Stanley asked.

"Molly made me a chocolate chip pancake," Rod said. "Want some?"

"I don't like anything sweet, Rod," Stanley said, dumping half of the scrambled eggs onto his plate and covering it in salt. Stanley was a salty guy, and applied that to everything, literally.

"Pa, could I go into town and meet-up with Glenn today?" Rod asked.

"Molly, what do you think?" Stanley asked. "Are you okay with your brother running out on you all day?"

"Rod, you can go," Sally said.

"You know, Glenn's been at the sheriff's station for entire days at a time, so I could go later tonight."

"There you go," Stanley said.

"Thanks, Rod," Molly said.

They all finished their breakfast and Rod and Molly went outside with Sunny. Sally sat on the porch and enjoyed the clear sky that day. Rod and Molly played fetch with Sunny. Stanley went back to sleep.

After almost an entire afternoon of playing fetch with Sunny, he ran onto the porch and collapsed in front of Sally so he could get a belly-rub from her. Sally sat down on the actual porch and gave him what he wanted.

"Can we go see the sunset, Rod?" Molly asked. "From the forest?"

"Ma, Molly wants to go into the forest to see the sunset," Rod shouted.

Rod wasn't worried about getting Sally's okay; it was Stanley that he was worried about. Stanley never liked it when Rod took Molly into the forest. The vast landscape was pretty dangerous to begin with, and he didn't want Rod to lose track of his young sister. Rod also didn't want to have to answer to Stanley for something happening to Molly.

"Go ahead," Sally said. "Just be careful, but have fun."

"Have you ever heard that from papa?" Molly asked, walking into the forest while holding Rod's hand.

"Not once," Rod said.

"I have a pretty good idea that you know where you're going," Molly said to Rod.

"I've got a great place for us to catch the sunset," Rod assured her. "But, before that happens, we're gonna have some fun."

Rod took Molly climbing trees, swimming, and rock climbing. Molly barely did any of that on her own; she spent a lot of time hanging onto Rod's back.

Once Molly was exhausted from the excitement that she usually never experienced, Rod took her to the base of a hill that changed right into a big lake.

"Have I ever told you that you're the best big brother in the West?" Molly asked, resting her head on Rod's shoulder.

"Just the West?" Rod asked. "What about the whole country?"

"I bet the New York big brothers take their baby-girls to Broadway to see a show," Molly said. "Just foolin'."

"I thought of that, but pa taught me about what happened to Lincoln and I wanted to give my sister something a little more under control," Rod said.

"Well, thank you," Molly said. "And I specified the West because you can't get better than the American West."

Molly was fixated on the orange-shadowed sunset. Rod wasn't moved by the display to begin with, but he was more focused on scoping for wolves, foxes and Apaches.

"Isn't it beautiful, Rod?" Molly asked him.

"I can't figure out what it is about stuff like this that has an effect on you ladies," Rod said.

"That's because you're out here every day baking in the hot sun."

"You think the sun's out when pa and I are working?" Rod asked, laughing. "Good one."

Rod snapped to attention when he thought he saw a pair of Indians in the brush across the lake. He started to hear that speaking to each other, and he clearly saw one of them tie a huge arrowhead to a big staff.

"Holy hell," Rod said.

"What is it?" Molly asked, sitting up with him.

"I think we've got some hostiles ahead," Rod said.

One of the Apaches looked at him.

"We need to go," Rod said, standing up. "Fast."

"Well, I can't keep up with you," Molly whispered.

Rod picked her up and ran as fast he could back to the farm. They made it without seemingly being pursued by the Apaches. When Rod came back, he felt like he ran into an even more dangerous situation. Stanley was on the porch with Sally.

"What do you got?" Stanley bellowed. "Gator? Bear?"

"Apaches," Rod said, bringing Molly right up to the porch and putting her down.

"How many were there?" Stanley asked Rod.

"I saw two," Rod said. "At least two."

"Rod, you may still go into town if you like," Stanley said, walking into the house.

"With the Indians about?" Molly asked.

"The path to town isn't that way," Sally said to Molly.

Stanley came back outside with a rifle, a shotgun and a revolver. He handed the revolver to Rod.

"For goodness sake, Stanley," Sally said, hugging Molly.

"Get inside," Stanley said, cocking the shotgun. "And take the damn fur-ball with you."

Sally and Molly took Sunny back into the house. One thing that Stanley hated about Sunny was that he was an awful guard dog. Sunny was just a lap dog that was born to play with people. He had no trace of aggression in him.

"Is this for Indians?" Rod asked, putting the gun away.

"Indians, rowdies at the tavern," Stanley said, sitting down with the shotgun in one hand and the rifle in the other.

"I don't mind you and Glenn going into the bar every now and then, just don't take part in all the shenanigans."

"I won't," Rod said, relieved. "Thanks, pa."

"Uh-huh," Stanley muttered, scoping the forest for the Indians.

It was really tough for Rod to have a real conversation with Stanley. In fact, it was hard for any of the McGillis' to have a real conversation with Stanley. If it didn't have to do with war or hunting, he really had no interest, and it showed.

Stanley usually let Rod go into town. He also usually let him go into the town's bar. Stanley believed in letting boys learn life lessons early on. But, he was unbelievably straight-laced. He could hold his liquor so well, he never got drunk. And that made him resent anyone that did get drunk, especially in public.

Rod walked down an open road toward town. The sun hadn't completely set yet, so Rod wasn't too nervous about being trailed by Indians in the night.

Rod strolled into town and saw that the night shift was already starting. Most of the people were making their way to the local tavern. Rod couldn't find his friend in the crowd.

Rod approached two sheriff deputies who were leaving the station.

"Is Glenn Wilson on duty today?" Rod asked them.

"Yeah, he is," one of them said. "He'll be there for a while, though."

Rod walked against the current of people toward the sheriff's station. He passed by a deputy asleep on a chair outside of the station. He had a big double-barrel shotgun across his lap.

Rod walked into the station to find another deputy sitting around drinking while a tall, skinny sixteen-year-old with a big bush of curly, black hair was mopping up the floor of the station.

"Hey, Glenn," Rod said.

"Hey, Rod," Glenn muttered. "Sir, am I almost done here?"

"Uh….."

The deputy stood up with buckling knees. He went to put his beer on the desk nearest him, but the bottle spilled onto the floor.

"I wouldn't bet on it," the deputy said, grabbing onto the desk to stay upright. "Don't forget to lock up."

"What?" Glenn asked.

"Time for you to man-up," the deputy said, stumbling out of the station.

Glenn looked over at the cells in the station. A prisoner threw his food-tray at the bars and got his scraps all over the floor around his cell.

"Aw, come on, damn," Glenn whined.

"Let me out," the prisoner said.

Glenn dipped his mop into a bucket of water, walked over to the cell and shook the excess water at the prisoner. The prisoner had no reaction.

"I don't know why you do it," Rod commented.

"Don't go there, Rod," Glenn pleaded, continuing to mop.

Glenn Wilson and Rod were best friends ever since they were young kids. Glenn's father and Stanley McGillis both served in the same unit during the Civil War. Glenn's father returned to Wyoming to be Ralph Hatcher's predecessor as the head sheriff of Wyoming; the sheriff at the capitol. It seemed impossible, but Glenn's father was even harder on Glenn than Stanley was on Rod.

Ever since Glenn's father became the sheriff, he wanted Glenn to follow in his footsteps. Glenn had been working as something of a go-boy in the department ever since he was old enough to think. Glenn's father gave the deputies a lot of discretion in how they treated Glenn, and they treated him extremely lousy. None of their treatment toward him was constructive. Glenn developed a very low self-esteem and had an impulse to let people walk over him. It was opposite with Rod and Stanley; Stanley taught Rod respect and self-building, and Rod felt like a confident and self-reliant person with a lot of self-respect, and tremendous respect for his father.

"I'll leave it alone, then," Rod said. "I'll take care of the pig-sty over there."

"Thank you," Glenn said.

Glenn was always very tightly-wound. He could never enjoy himself because he was brought-up in an environment where he was always being given work to do. Glenn was never relaxed by the fact that he finished a job because he was on his toes to start another one.

"Molly and I ran into some Apache warriors as the sun was setting," Rod said.

"Hot damn!" Glenn said. "She should have appreciated the excitement."

"I got her out of there as quick as I could," Rod said.

"Apaches, huh?" the prisoner asked Rod. "Next time you've got to hang 'em from their damn totem poles."

"Did Mr. McGillis rail you for taking Molly into Indian territory?" Glenn asked.

"Right now, he's probably setting-up for a shot at one of 'em."

"Okay, we're finished," Glenn said, putting the mop supplies in the cleaning closet. "Let's hit the bar."

Glenn locked-up the station and he and Rod walked across town to the bar. Everyone was there. Glenn and Rod sat down at the counter and looked at the rest of the scene. It wasn't an overly-rowdy crowd; just a bunch of people unwinding after a day of hard work.

"Real salt-to-the-earth people?" Glenn asked Rod.

"Oh yeah," Rod said, nodding.

"I figured no one would know better than you," Glenn said. "I mean that in a good way."

"Sure," Rod said, understanding.

"Hey, look who's here," Glenn said, nudging his head across the bar. "And look at who she's eye-ballin'."

Rod looked across the bar and saw in a corner, there was a particularly aloof group of people that looked like they belonged on the east coast, owning factories. They were rich advisors to the governor. There was also the governor's beautiful niece, and she was looking at Rod.

The governor's niece was the same age as Rod and Glenn. She had long blonde hair with curls in scattered spots. She had pale skin like Molly's because she never got out in the sun much. She had sad, brown eyes because it wasn't a happy life living with the governor. Rod thought her depressed expression was attractive for some reason.

When Beverly Roth saw Rod look over at her, she got nervous and looked away.

"Do I have to sit here?" Beverly asked one of the men.

"Where else are you going to go?" one of them asked, puffing cigar smoke at her. She coughed a little bit.

"Everywhere else looks more fun than this corner," she complained.

"The governor wouldn't like it if we let his niece mingle with the scum of Wyoming," another one of them said.

"He didn't even want me in the mansion this weekend," she said. "What makes you think he cares?"

"Not much," another man said. "He's about to be rid of you for two weeks."

"When does Hatcher return?" Rod asked Glenn. "My pa's anxious to pay the new round of taxes."

"This week," Glenn said, not happy. "I like it much better when he's after Butler and Rhodes."

"I take it you root for Rhodes," Rod said, "on account of Rhodes is able to keep Hatcher on the road for months at a time. Butler is always a sitting duck."

"Butler's a sheriff's dream of an outlaw," Glenn explained. "Never able to do too much damage, never able to get away in time. Rhodes, though, is a nightmare of an outlaw to the sheriff. He's slick, does a lot of damage, and people like him."

"Yeah, I understand he's a real hotshot."

"I'll tell you about a hotshot," Glenn said. "Beverly Roth is a hotshot."

"Why would she ever go for someone like us, Glenn?"

"Not us," Glenn said. "She would never go for me. It's you she'd go for."

"I don't think so, Glenn. I'm a simple country boy that handles a farm. That's probably not good enough for the niece of the governor, and someone as aristocratic as Roth. I don't think she's into guys like us, or, me."

Governor Roth

The sitting governor of Wyoming had two governor's mansions. There was the governor's mansion in the capital, and then the mansion that the governor owned. The governor was supposed to have only one mansion, but he accumulated a lot of wealth since the beginning of his term, and he didn't count on that term ending.

As he usually was, Governor Nolan Roth was sitting in the official governor's mansion with his feet up on his polished oak desk, a cigar in his mouth, a suit on his body, and his slick, black hair combed over to the side with 3 big curls on the right side of his forehead. Governor Roth was a very clean, rich person and always liked to present himself that way.

There was a knock on his door. He removed the cigar from his mouth with a hand that included a finger with an enormous ring on it

"It's open," he said, with an accent that was naturally Western but forced into a bland sound.

The door opened and a deputy walked in.

"Your niece is on a train south right now, governor," the deputy said.

"Niece?" Nolan asked.

"Beverly," the deputy answered.

"Oh, right, right," Nolan said, putting the cigar back in his mouth.

"By the way, I got the latest edition of the paper in."

The deputy pulled a newspaper out of his coat and handed it to the governor. Nolan laid it out on his desk and looked at the cover story. There was a photo of a few dead deputies on the ground in the town that Derek Rhodes and his gang had just robbed.

When Nolan saw this, he crushed his cigar in his hand. The deputy went over and swept the ashes away.

"I can't believe this," Nolan said, grinding his teeth. "Derek Rhodes is really starting to piss me off."

"That picture is not accurate, governor," the deputy said. "There were many more dead deputies in view, but they moved them out of the camera's view. You know, to cover-up the mess."

"For goodness sake," Nolan said, sighing. "Look at this headline. 'Outlaw Derek Rhodes and his gang still at large'. I can't take much more of this. Neither can the state of Wyoming. Where is Ralph? Has he returned yet?"

"Not yet, sir," the deputy said. "I have the spokesman for the Vanderbilt railroad company ready to speak with you."

"Send him in," Nolan said.

As the deputy went to retrieve the business executive for the Vanderbilt railroad company, Nolan took two glasses and a bottle of Brandy out of his desk and poured the two glasses. He also took out his cigar case to offer to the Vanderbilt spokesman. Nolan was always happy to share the benefits of high society with other members of high society.

The deputy returned with a man in a suit like Nolan's.

"Thank you, deputy," Nolan said, flipping him a coin. "Keep an eye out for the Sheriff."

The deputy left the governor's office.

"Have a seat," Nolan said to the executive, "sample one of these cigars and share some of my liquor with me."

"Gladly," the Vanderbilt spokesman said, taking a cigar from Nolan and Nolan lit it for him. Then, the spokesman took a sip of the Brandy.

"If you don't mind me saying," the spokesman said, "your accent doesn't have the Western twang that we all hear about in New York."

"That's because, unfortunately, everyone in New York sees a ragtag, pathetic cowboy when they hear the Western twang. I simply am better than that."

"Well put, governor," the spokesman said.

"I am sorry to hear about Cornelius' condition," Nolan said. "It's a shame when success goes on the decline."

"Well, it's obvious what he has set-up for his company's future, the spokesman said. "He knows which of his sons will be taking over."

"I understand that you would like to build a railroad through my territory," Nolan said. "I just might be certain I'm going to let you do that."

"Really?" the spokesman asked, relieved and surprised. "Just like that? I haven't even given you the construction plan yet."

"Let me take a look at it," Nolan said.

The spokesman took a folder with papers in it out of a case he had with him. The cover of the folder had the engraved logo of the Vanderbilt railroad company on it.

"It's a good looking folder," Nolan said. "I tell you one thing; there are a lot of conditions if I'm going to let the DC government intrude on my boundaries, but I'm always ready to let the privately wealthy to make some more money."

Nolan skimmed through the railroad construction blueprints and the contract between the Vanderbilt Company and the government of Wyoming.

"You want us to provide security forces during construction" Nolan asked.

"Yes," the spokesman said. "The son that Cornelius frowns upon of late had the idea of training the workers to be their own security. He got laughed out of that meeting."

"I'm sure," Nolan said, taking out a pen. He signed the contract.

"I will take this back to my bosses and see what they think," the spokesman said. "Keep this map for your reference."

The spokesman handed Nolan a copy of the map of the proposed railroad. Nolan looked at the intended path and laughed with malice.

"We may need to be cutting through some Indian territory," the spokesman said.

Nolan started to bellow.

"That's precisely what we're going to do!" he boasted.

"I think we may need to tour the current plan to see what we're dealing with… land-wise."

"Absolutely not," Nolan said, leaning up close to the spokesman. "I have been waiting for an excuse to clear-out more Indians, and this looks like it's going to be a big-sweep."

"I'm glad to help out," the spokesman said, a little taken aback by the governor's excitement at dispersing Indians. He wasn't used to that kind of pleasure in New York, where he was from.

"This is perfect," Nolan said, walking up to the map of his state and comparing it to the railroad plan.

"This railroad is going to go right through an Apache camp that has been a real pain in the ass," Nolan said, excitedly. "I can't wait to see them scatter and high-tail it into whatever forest is left in my state."

Nolan turned to the spokesman with a grin.

"The security for the railroad is all taken care of," Nolan assured. "My top sheriff is the best in the business. The title of my ethics code for my sheriff's department is 'shoot first, ask questions later'."

Nolan started laughing suggestively. The spokesman started to laugh, too, but with a lot of reserve. Nolan was kind of scaring him.

"I tell you what," Nolan said, putting the map on his desk. "Before you leave to go back to New York, why don't we have a round of croquet?"

"That sounds fine," the spokesman said.

Nolan was a big fan of upper-class activities like croquet, drinking excessively-expensive liquor, and he aspired to go to see plays in theatres. He also liked to do these things with other rich people. Another thing he liked was abusing the office of governor as badly as he could and the sheriff's department. The other half of the tax money that Nolan didn't embezzle for himself funded Hatcher's men to terrorize Wyoming into submission to Nolan's ridiculous tax rates.

What Nolan didn't like the rustic, backwoods culture of the people in Wyoming with less money, and he wasn't particularly all that proud of the American West. He didn't like hunting, trapping, explorers, ranchers, people that work in mines, people that work on railroads, Indians, and cowboys. But, he liked pawning poor people off to massacre Indians or to de-forest. Nolan did like, however, the businessmen who profited from the railroads and mines. Nolan had to be the coldest governor to ever serve.

In addition to being an awful governor, Nolan was a worse uncle. Nolan took Beverly in because his brother's mine went under and his brother lost everything. Nolan liked his brother when he had his money, but once Nolan's brother lost it all, Nolan lost all respect for him. Nolan had a sick view of the American work-ethic belief.

But, even Nolan wasn't cruel enough to let a little girl suffer in poverty. However, Nolan didn't have to like doing good for a kid, and he made sure Beverly knew he didn't want her around. He constantly treated her to reiterate his feelings toward her. He constantly ignored and neglected her, but his favorite thing to do was send her south to see her parents so he could get rid of her. Nolan's role as an uncle to Beverly was more of a pathetic charade than anything sincere. He only took Beverly in so his recently bankrupt brother would not ask him for money.

A few days after the Vanderbilt railroad companies left Wyoming, Sheriff Ralph Hatcher and what was left of his deputies returned. It was perfect timing, because the governor was about to give a speech to a rally of people in front of the governor's mansion. It was a very rare congregation of non-government citizens; they all supported Nolan.

Nolan's only true support came from the office of governor, less than 3 percent of people in Wyoming that were rich, and the sheriff's department, and conservative, old citizens. Nolan deliberately catered to the needs of the rich and of the sheriff's department. Nolan was very safe as governor with the armed forces of Wyoming behind him, and with the money behind them. A little less than the other half of tax money that Nolan didn't embezzle for himself went to the sheriff's department. And, all the tax money was generated from the poor in Wyoming at ridiculous rates. But, there was nothing any of the citizens of Wyoming could do to try and change the actions of the governor. They were all terrified of Ralph and his men. Democracy was more than totally suspended in all areas of Wyoming since the beginning of Nolan's term. There wasn't even a state legislature anymore; Nolan ordered Ralph and the sheriff's department to massacre the legislatures and burn down the chambers.

The truth was, the sheriff's department and office of governor wasn't corrupt before Nolan and Ralph. But, once old-man Wilson stepped down and was succeeded by Ralph Hatcher, everything changed. This event coincided with Nolan's sweeping election, and then everything in Wyoming's government turned dirty and crooked. In fact, Nolan and Ralph were in cahoots from the very beginning.

Ralph went inside the governor's mansion while the rest of the capitol deputies fought the crowd back.

Nolan was looking at himself in a mirror to try and look as good as he could to stick it to the poor people.

"Governor, about the press…." Ralph said with a lot of shame.

"Don't worry about it," Nolan said, turning around and greeting his friend, the sheriff. "I'm pretty close to burning down the entire state to smoke Rhodes out," Nolan said.

"It wouldn't be a big loss," Ralph said. "The only places of wealth in this state are here, the department, and a few mansions on the east. It would be a great idea to purge this place of the scum poor."

"Let me go lie my ass off to the people of Wyoming to save ours yet again."

Ralph followed Nolan out of the mansion and onto a platform that was set-up for Nolan's speech. The deputies made a wall of themselves in front of the platform for security. Ralph stood on the platform next to Nolan for effect. Nolan was standing behind a podium with a steel-plated seal of Wyoming's office of governor.

Nolan observed his crowd as he figured out what he wanted to say to them. All of them were men and women over sixty years of age. It was the demographic of citizens that believed anything the executive did was for the better and that all the harshness of the sheriff's department was to keep the "rowdy, young mob" in check.

"Well, I thank you all for coming today," Nolan said, smiling at everyone with no sincerity in his eyes. "I'm proud of everyone for refusing to be silent at the mob's request. They think they are the majority, those who don't approve of me or sheriff Hatcher…"

A big wave of "boos" arose from the crowd. They liked Ralph as sheriff a lot.

"And there are those who complain about my tax rates…."

Even louder "boos."

"But, they're just that stupid if they can't figure out that the taxes help honorable public servants like Sheriff Hatcher and his good deputies to keep this city safe, and all of you seniors protected from the riff-raff!"

That brought a huge applause from the crowd. Ralph nudged Nolan to get his attention and asked if he could step up and speak. Nolan was accommodating.

"As your sheriff, I want to assure all of you that just because the outlaw Derek Rhodes…"

Ralph was immediately cut-off by real angry "boos" and mean shouts from the crowd. They hated Derek and his gang.

"Yeah, I'm with ya'll," Ralph said. The crowd laughed.

"On a serious note, though," Ralph backtracked, "He just narrowly got away from us in an Eastern city. He is not a threat who live within the boundaries of the governor's mansion, but we in the sheriff's department are a serious threat to him and will continue to be a threat to him as long as we have your terrific support!"

The crowd applauded Ralph's words. Nolan nudged him out of the way and spoke again.

"Thus begins a new month of prosperity for Wyoming," he said.

"Governor!" an old woman shouted, sticking her hand up in the air.

"Yes, mam," Nolan said, pointing her out.

"When will the next election be?" she asked. "We want to know when to vote for you again."

Everyone else nodded and muttered in agreement.

"Let me be absolutely clear," Nolan said sternly, "there will be no more elections in my lifespan. As long as I am I alive, I will be governor."

The applause started to start. "And good things will be on the way for Wyoming!"

Nolan and Ralph went inside the governor's mansion as the crowd appreciatively applauded their governor and sheriff. The younger deputies were a little nervous about the governor disbanding all governor elections for the rest of his life. That was as unconstitutional as it could get.

Nolan was an economic governor in everyone's eyes. He was obsessed with money, having money, supporting people who had it, and leaving people in the dust who didn't have it. Everyone in Wyoming, rich and poor alike, assumed that it was the economy that Nolan most cared about as governor. Whether people thought he was fixing it or destroying it was a different argument. But, he was definitely destroying it.

Only Nolan and Ralph knew what the top political issue on their agenda was. That was outlaws and law enforcement. Enforcement of unjust laws, to be exact. And more specifically, the outlaw that they were most concerned about was Derek Rhodes and his men.

It wasn't helping Nolan's case at all that he wouldn't admit the growing number of outlaws in Wyoming was because of him expanding the poor and homeless numbers in the state.

Derek Rhodes was everything that Nolan hated about the West: underprivileged, unsophisticated, rustic, folksy, liked the outdoors, and he rounded-up anti-Nolan sentiment like nobody's business. But, the most frustrating thing about Derek to Nolan was that he was good. Nolan had taken measure after measure to try and bring Derek to "justice" and each measure got more hard-nosed as they went along. But, nothing was working. Nolan was just about getting fed-up with Derek.

"Here's what we're going to do," Nolan said, leading Ralph out the back door of the governor's mansion and toward the city jail, "we're going to get the new batch of prisoners to talk."

"My deputies have been trying, governor," Ralph said. "They're too stubborn."

Nolan stopped and turned to Ralph. He patted him on the shoulder.

"You're too soft, Ralph," Nolan said, chuckling. "You've got to get a little tougher around the edges."

Ralph thought that was bizarre criticism; Ralph was regarded as truly the nastiest person in Wyoming. Nolan had never actually physically harmed anyone, but Ralph had, many times.

Nolan and Ralph walked into the city jail and up to the cells of a few cowboys that had been locked-up.

"You, there," Ralph said to a deputy, "bring this one out for us."

He deputy opened up the cell that Ralph pointed at and dragged the prisoner out.

"I didn't do nothing," the cowboy snapped as Ralph and the deputy brought him into a room that was like a medieval torture chamber.

"As much as I'd love to stay and you guys tear his limbs out of the sockets," Nolan said, "I've got things to do."

"Don't worry about a thing, governor," Ralph said as they chained the guy to a wall with his back facing them. "We've got it under control."

Nolan walked out of the room and made his way out the jail. As he left, he could hear Ralph and the deputy whipping the prisoner and the prisoner was screaming in pain. That made Nolan instinctively smile.

"Where is Rhodes' hideout?" Ralph shouted. "Where do they hide?"

The McGillis' troubles

It had been another duration of a three-month crime-spree for Derek and his men, so it was the beginning of a two-month span of returning to their regular lives.

Tom returned to his wife and young, young daughter in Nevada. If there was anyone in Derek's gang that was able to scrounge-up a regular life, Tom was the closest. Derek had met Tom's wife and his daughter when she was too young to realize Derek's poor behavior. Derek noticed that having a wife and daughter made Tom calm down and act like a normal person, not the neurotic nutcase that annoyed everyone on the crime-sprees. Derek assumed that everyone was a better father and family-man than him, and he thought Tom was the best. But, he was the best on any normal-person standards of family and parenting.

The other semi-family man in the group was Tex. He had a big, big Texan family with a lot of people and they were all big people. Derek had spent a Thanksgiving with them once. They were all just like Tex. They were all tall, thick, curly-haired, loud and liked to laugh.

Other than that, Derek, Villegas, Otis, Surge and Marcus all just kind of wandered for the two months off. Marcus always stayed close to someone because he was too young to be on his own. Villegas always stayed around the border of Mexico. Surge made a little extra money helping people on the street for money. He was good at working like that; he was a field medic during the Civil War. So, he had to be able to just start operating on people under pressure and without preparation. That made him really good.

Otis had half-brothers and step-family members scattered over the old South, so he bounced around their homes.

Derek loved to reside inside Wyoming's state capitol on his time off. He was never really off from being an outlaw; he continued to pickpocket sheriff deputies and obvious bureaucrats. He figured that he would continue to stay so close to the governor and sheriff until they caught on to his act. Derek could stand by any wanted poster of himself for as long as he wanted, and nobody would ever call him out. Derek was such a folk hero to everyone in Wyoming that they would brave the sheriff's torture methods to not rat-out their man.

Rod felt weird that morning. He slept up until the exact moment that Stanley would come into his room to see if he was awake and ready to go to work for the day. Stanley never showed up, even after Rod waited.

Curious as to what was going on, and assuming that Stanley was waiting downstairs for him, Rod got dressed and walked downstairs. He found Stanley sitting at the kitchen table looking at some post that was for him. He didn't look happy about it.

"Are you ready to go, pop?" Rod asked. Stanley paused for a moment.

"I've got some important stuff to take care of," Stanley grunted. "In a minute."

"What do you got?" Rod asked, sitting down next to him.

"It's the latest bill from the creditors that loaned us the money for the farm," Stanley explained. "The bill is exceedingly higher than the last one."

"Can they do that?" Rod asked. "They can't do that."

"Nobody likes a complainer, Rod," Stanley said. "We have to pay our bills. Here's a good lesson for you, kid. Don't ask people for favors if you can't pay them back."

That made sense to Rod.

Once Stanley was finished getting the money together for the bill, he and Rod went to work feeding the livestock, checking the fishing net (nothing at all that morning) hunting, and checking the traps. Stanley was in a particularly ornery mood because they got nothing from the fishing net and none of the traps caught anything. They couldn't even find any animals to hunt.

Rod wasn't all that surprised that they weren't crossing any animals; Stanley's yelling and shouting in anger was probably scaring them all away. But, Stanley was the last guy that anyone wanted to tell to calm down.

Just as Stanley was about to tell Rod that they were giving up, a huge grizzly bear burst out of the woods and in between them.

"Rod, stay calm!" Stanley yelled.

Easy for Stanley to say; the bear was on its hind legs, staring right at Rod and roaring loudly. Each time Rod would step back, the bear would furiously swipe its claws at him.

"Hey!" Stanley shouted, trying to get the bears attention.

The bear turned to him and got on all fours. It wound its body up as if to spring at Stanley. Rod put a big Winchester round into the bear's rear end. The bear spun around and started to charge at Rod. Before Rod turned to run, he shot at the bear and missed. He wasn't really taking his time to aim. The bear smacked the gun out of his hands and Rod turned around to run. He got a few steps in before the bear used its paw to smack him down at the shoulder. Rod tumbled down to the ground and rolled over before the bear landed on him. Rod started slashing at the bear with his big bowie knife.

Stanley ran over to the bear and whacked him over the head with his crutch. That was the first time Rod ever saw him use both his legs.

The bear forgot about Rod and clawed Stanley in the chest. Stanley was knocked back into a tree. While the bear was distracted, Rod shoved the knife into the bear's throat and pulled it out so the bear could lose blood. The bear drove Rod to the ground again and batted his face with its paw. There was a loud gunshot and Rod saw blood pour out of the bear's throat and head. Stanley was standing on both feet and clutching a smoking revolver. He shot the bear in the temple again and the bear died.

"I appreciate that, pa," Rod said, "but could you help me get this bear off of me?"

"Sure thing," Stanley said, picking up his crutch and pushing the bear off of Rod with it.

"It was female," Stanley said, starting to get a little wobbly. "That's why she was so aggressive."

"Are you okay, pop?" Rod asked.

Stanley started to cough.

"Pa?" Rod asked, nervously.

Stanley started to have really nasty-sounding, dry coughs. He started to vomit a little bit, and he collapsed.

"Pa!" Rod yelled, trying to give him a hand.

"I don't need no help, boy," Stanley barked, waving Rod away from him. "I can take care of myself. I took care of myself with Johnny 'Rebs, Indians and beasts like that after me every day."

Rod and Stanley walked back toward the farm, with Stanley choking and throwing-up the whole way. Rod tried not to cry, but he had to release a few tears at the sight and sound of his father breaking down. His war injuries were catching up him.

When they walked into the house, it didn't take long for Sally and Molly to come running over to see what was the matter.

"Stanley, are you okay?" Sally shouted.

"I'm fine!" Stanley barked, trying to get up the stairs.

"Lay down, pa," Rod suggested.

"I can handle this, ya'll people!" Stanley yelled, disappearing in his room.

"What happened?" Molly asked Rod with tears in her eyes. She was allowed to cry in front of Stanley; Stanley wasn't going to ever criticize her for not being a man.

"This bear attacked us," Rod began.

"Oh my God, are you okay?" Sally shouted, hugging Rod.

"I'm fine, ma," Rod said. "Don't worry about me. The bear had me pinned down and pa…."

"THE BEAR HAD YOU PINNED DOWN?" Sally asked, grabbing his shoulders. "You said not to worry about you!"

"And you shouldn't," Rod said. He was really more concerned about Stanley right then.

"And pa shot the bear with his gun. I guess he had one too many smoke clouds that he breathed in and it got to him. Oh yeah, he was on both feet."

"Your father was on both feet?" Sally asked in awe. "He hasn't been on both feet since the war…."

"You're sure you're okay?" Molly asked, hugging Rod.

"Yes, I'm okay," Rod said.

"Good," Molly said. She punched Rod's arm.

"Why'd you let this happen to papa?" she joked.

Sally and Rod laughed.

"Rod, get on up here," Stanley shouted.

Rod ran upstairs and into Stanley's room. Stanley was lying in his bed resting.

"What do you need, pa?" Rod asked. "I'll do anything you ask me."

"There's a rodeo today in the city," Stanley gasped. "Take Molly to see it and while you're at it, mail the bank's bill."

"Sure thing," Rod said.

Rod walked downstairs and passed Molly and Sally.

"What did he want?" Sally asked.

"He wants me to send his bill to the bank," Rod said, putting the bill in his pocket, "and to take Molly to see the rodeo."

"Yay," Molly said, excitedly.

"Have fun," Sally encouraged as Molly got on Rod's back. "I'm sure your father will be fine."

Rod walked to the door, and there was a knock before he opened it. He opened the door for sheriff Hatcher and a deputy. Sheriff Hatcher had never shown-up at the farm before. Rod was glad now that he saw him.

"Tax day, boy," Ralph barked. "Where's the man of the house."

"He's the man of the house right now," Sally said, coldly. She wasn't as trusting of the sheriff's department as Stanley was.

"He's sick in bed right now," Rod said to Ralph. "He doesn't have time for this."

Ralph bent over a little bit so he could be at eye-level with Rod; Ralph was so tall that he was taller than Rod, Stanley and Sally. Once Ralph's face got close to Rod and Molly's, Rod could feel Molly's grip tighten on his shoulder because she was so scared of the sheriff. He wasn't even looking at her.

"Let me explain something to your young head, kid," Ralph said to Rod. "The whole purpose behind the governor's taxes is that we have the resources to keep Indians and outlaws from assaulting people like yourself. So why don't you show a little damn gratitude?"

"Rod, don't bother the sheriff!" Stanley shouted, trying to make it down the stairs.

"Pa, you shouldn't be up," Rod said.

"We'll handle this, Stan," Sally said.

"Would everyone quit worrying," Stanley muttered, walking up to the sheriff with a small sack of coins.

"Here you are, sheriff," Stanley said to Ralph, graciously. "I trust this year will be another strong year for the sheriff against the riff-raff."

"Quarter?" the deputy asked. "The tax rates will be collected quarterly now."

"The current rates?" Rod shouted.

"The boy's right," Ralph said to his deputy. "The current rates are much too low. Good thing the governor decided to raise them."

"Don't worry about a thing, sheriff," Stanley said. "I'll teach the boy civic duty."

"That's an option," Ralph said. "But, you should work on yourself a little. You look less appealing than a cow-pie."

Ralph and the deputy left the far laughing. They were right, though. Stanley's face was ghost-pale and he had bags under his eyes.

"Pa, you can't let those guys push you around like that," Rod said.

"That wasn't pushing around," Stanley said. "That was a necessity. There are a lot of things the government does that you don't realize you like. You best understand this, too, Molly. Without the government, there'd be no one to pay my benefits from fighting with the Union army, no one to pay my injured soldier's medical bills, people could walk into any farm they want and take whatever they liked. Axes pay for all that good stuff."

"I get it, pa," Rod said.

"Please go rest," Sally said to Stanley. "This excitement isn't helping you."

Stanley made his way upstairs, mumbling about he could take care of himself.

"Mama, we'll stay if you need help taking care of papa," Molly said.

"Yeah," Rod said. "We don't have to go into the city."

"You **are** going into the city to send your father's bill out and you will go to the rodeo and have a good time. If your father won't accept any help from you, that's that. He's my problem, now."

If it had been Sally or Molly that was sick, Stanley wouldn't let Rod even think about anything else except taking care of them. But, the girls would have been much more welcoming to care. Stanley was too stubborn and proud to get any treatment from his family.

Rod and Molly got to the city really early so Rod could take care of Stanley's bank bill and get good seats at the rodeo. They went to the sheriff's station first to see if Glenn could hook them up with anything. Glenn was actually prepared to give them an insider advantage.

"Rod, I've got great news!" Glenn shouted happily as he saw them. "Hey, Molly."

"Hi, Glenn," Molly said. Outside of Rod, Stanley and Sally, Glenn was Molly's only friend.

"Seriously, though," Glenn said, "I got assigned to the section right where they let the bull out. You and Molly can sit right up front! What do you think?"

"That sounds terrific," Rod said. "Molly?"

"Thanks, Glenn!" Molly exclaimed.

Rod was about to turn around to go to the arena, but someone big and strong bumped into him on purpose and went right over to Glenn. It was Ralph. He grabbed Glenn by the shirt collar and slammed him onto a desk.

"Listen up, Glenn-Willie," Ralph said to him. Glenn-Willie was Ralph's nickname for Glenn.

"I hear you've got a fancy security assignment at the rodeo," Ralph said. "This is no gift. This is important. If you screw this up, you're going to be scrubbing prison cells."

"I already scrub prison cells," Glenn said.

"Well, you'll be doing it for the rest of your life if you screw this job up," Ralph said.

Ralph let go of Glenn and walked out of the station, bumping into Rod on purpose again.

"He showed up at the farm and robbed us this morning," Rod told Glenn.

"Yeah, he probably did," Glenn said. "Did you hear that the current annual tax rates are now going to be collected quarterly?"

"Yeah, we heard about that scam," Molly said.

"Hey, enough with being down in the dumps," Rod said. "Show us these unbelievable seats we're hearing about."

"Oh, right," Glenn said. "You're going to love them. Follow me."

Glenn took Rod and Molly into the rodeo arena through a restricted entrance so they could avoid the big crowd. Glenn brought them to two seats that were right above the gate where they let the bull out. The cowboy wasn't out yet, but the bull was already strapped-up. Molly never sat down; she just stood at the railing and started at the bull the whole time. It was the biggest animal she had ever seen in her life.

The rodeo proceedings officially begun when the governor and Ralph appeared in the governor's private box-seats in the arena. The overwhelming majority of the crowd was anti-Roth, so the booing and negative shouts were much louder than the appreciative cheers. There were too few rich people to hear their applause, and the old people didn't have the lung capacity to shout like the poor masses.

Ralph took out his big revolver and shot near a crowd to shut them up. Scattered deputies shot just overhead of their sections to calm the people down.

"I wish you were sheriff, Glenn," Molly said, finally looking away from the bull. "You wouldn't be mean like Hatcher."

"No, I wouldn't" Glenn said. "Everything would be much different. Your father would actually have money to maintain your farm."

"Rod, what's he talking about?" Molly asked.

"Nothing," Rod said. "He's exaggerating."

When Molly looked back at the bull, Rod stomped on Glenn's foot.

"Ow, what was that for?" Glenn asked.

"She doesn't need to know about that," Rod whispered.

"She'll find out eventually. People are living in the woods more and more now-a-days, hasn't she noticed?"

"She doesn't get out much," Rod said.

The rider finally entered the bull's pen and got on. He was getting a lot of waves and cheers from everyone around the pen, but he took off his bandana and gave it specially to Molly. She was very happy about that.

Rod and Glenn noticed that the brim of the rider's hat was especially low on his face; it was almost as if he was trying to hide his face.

The rodeo clowns opened up the gate and released the bull and the rider. Molly got distracted by the clowns for a little bit. She didn't know how to appreciate the actual rodeo at that point in her life.

The rider was very, very good. The bull was notorious for being the toughest bull in Wyoming; no one lasted more than five seconds on it, and no one was able to walk out of the arena by themselves after riding it.

"Hey, this guy is good," Rod said to Glenn.

"I'm surprised people are still attempting to ride this one."

In the governor's private box, he and Ralph weren't as happy.

"Damn it," Nolan barked to Ralph. "I bet a lot of money that this guy would be a damn pancake in twenty seconds. He's broken the damn record by a long shot now."

"You want me to have my men seal-off the arena?" Ralph asked.

"That would be great," Nolan asked.

Ralph got up and went to go spread the word around not to let the rider out once he was finished. The rider noticed that he was about to be boxed in. So, he took a final victory lap around the arena and took his hat off, revealing that he was Derek Rhodes, Nolan's most wanted outlaw. Nolan sprang out of his seat when he saw him.

"Appreciate the opportunity for some fun, governor!" Derek shouted, putting the hat back on, this time not worrying about hiding his identity.

"Just give my winnings to my bookie!"

Nolan rubbed his forehead to try and deal with the stress at being tricked into losing a wager to Derek.

"You're trapped, Rhodes!" Ralph shouted, running to the front row of the arena.

"Wanna bet?" Derek yelled.

Derek's bull charged toward where Ralph was standing. Ralph thought Derek was just trying to scare him. It turned out, Derek was serious in his own humorous way.

Derek's bull launched itself into the seats and scattered everyone there, even the sheriff and his deputies. Derek used the opportunity of confusion to make his swift escape out of the arena. Ralph and the deputies started to fire at him as he ran, but they only managed to hit innocent bystanders. Molly really enjoyed all that excitement.

"Does that happen all the time?" Molly asked Glenn.

"Only involving Rhodes," Glenn said.

Rod was pretty bewildered, too, but not like Molly was. Rod actually wished that he had the nerve to stand up to the governor and sheriff like Rhodes did. His father's lessons of civic duty didn't seem like they were correct anymore.

When Rod and Molly returned home after the rodeo fiasco, at least, they didn't think of it as a fiasco like the governor and sheriff did, it was a very dreary day. Sally made them be very quiet so they wouldn't disturb Stanley, but they didn't need to be told that. They all just mostly played chess and checkers. Molly beat everyone many times; she was the smart one in the family. Stanley and Sally taught her how to read, write and do math. Rod was the maintenance part of the family. He knew how to hunt, fish, build, and ultimately take care of the farm. Stanley thought that was what any man needed to know in life.

At night, though, Stanley couldn't help but be woken up. An outlaw gang, not Derek's, had decided to ride through the farm and mess it up just for fun. Sally and Molly were hiding in her and Rod's room and Rod, against Sally and Molly's pleas, ran outside onto the porch with his shotgun. Sunny was in the room with Sally and Molly, but like usual, he was just lying there and wagging his tail like there was nothing wrong.

Rod walked outside to see the livestock slaughtered, the crops burned, and the barn torn down. It made Rod really mad that they did this for no reason; they didn't take anything and got nothing out of it.

Rod decided to start shooting. Hey were kind of far away and starting to ride off, so the shotgun wasn't working too well. Stanley angrily walked out next to Rod.

"Let me show you how it's done," Stanley said, lining up a shot on the last outlaw to ride away. Stanley took his time and just before the last outlaw was out of range, Stanley took a shot with his revolver and hit the outlaw right in the back of the head.

"Nice shot, pa," Rod said, watching the outlaw's body fall off his horse as it rode off with the gang.

"The shotgun…. Isn't good…. Damn…"

Stanley started to cough and collapse again.

"Are they gone?" Sally asked, running out with Molly.

"Oh, they destroyed everything!" Molly yelled, crying.

"Ma, tomorrow, we have to take pa to the doctor," Rod said.

"Yeah, I think so," Sally sighed.

The next day, Rod and Sally took Stanley to the town's doctor. They left Molly with Glenn at the sheriff's station. If something was really wrong with Stanley, they didn't want Molly to hear about it.

The truth was, there were many thing things really wrong with Stanley. He had the black lung for a long time because of all the smoke and led from the war, cuts he had from day-to-day work with Rod were infected badly, his broken leg never got sufficient treatment so it started to mess with other things in his body around it, and his mind was very off from surviving the harsh conditions of the war. The doctor said that his intense hatred of Indians, animals and Southerners was damaging him psychologically.

"So, what can you do, doc?" Stanley asked after the doctor explained all the problems.

"I wish you'd have noticed these symptoms much earlier in your life, Stan," the doctor said. "All this stuff is close to being irrevocable.

But, I can attempt to operate on you. Your psychological conditions… I would just try and urge you to relax."

"I tell him that all the time," Sally said.

"You've got to try the operation, pa," Rod insisted.

"Yes," Stanley said. "I think I'll go through with the operation."

"Okay," the doctor said, a little nervously. "After my diagnosis, I put together something of what I think would be a bill after all this…."

The doctor gulped as Stanley took it from him and looked at it. Rod saw something he never saw before: Stanley released a tear.

"This is a pretty big number, doc," Stanley said.

"I know," the doctor said, also upset by the price. "You see, the governor had mandated that all doctors raise their prices for medical services to keep up with the higher taxes. I have some more bad news. The governor has also just cut-off all Civil War benefits from Washington from coming into Wyoming."

Stanley sighed.

"I'm sorry," the doctor said, weakly.

"There's nothing you can do," Stanley said. "I understand."

"Ma, could I talk to you, please?" Rod asked.

"Sure," Sally said. "We'll be right back."

Sally and Rod walked out of the doctor's office.

"I can't let pa suffer through this just because we don't have the money," Rod said.

"I don't want this, either," Sally said, starting to cry. "But, what can we do?"

"I don't know yet," Rod said. "But I'm going to do something."

That night, Sally let Rod stay in the city that night. Rod and Glenn mostly just sat around the bar and drank. Rod was drinking much more than usual then.

"I heard about the governor cancelling all the Union benefits," Glenn said. 'He didn't so much as cancel them as have people in the sheriff's department stakeout the post offices and redirect them back to the governor's pocket."

"Pa has this belief that anything the government does is for the best," Rod said. "Now they're playing with his life, and he doesn't know what to do. I don't know what to do, either."

"I understand," Glenn said. "I wouldn't know what to do if my pa was in this situation."

"I can't let him deal with this," Rod said. "I need to do something."

Someone in a leather jacket and familiar cowboy hat sat down next to Rod at the counter.

"You sound like you're in kind of a pickle, kid," the guy said. The voice was very familiar.

"I sure am," Rod said, turning to the guy. He had the brim of his hat over his eyes.

"I hate to see people's lives get gambled by the government," the cowboy said. "It ain't right. It ain't right for people to depend on anybody but themselves."

"Who are you?" Rod asked.

The cowboy lifted the brim of his hat up and revealed his face. It was Derek.

"Ah," Glenn said, getting up. "Nothing personal, but I need to be very far away from this discussion."

Glenn left the bar. Nobody in the sheriff's department could find out he was around Derek Rhodes.

"I saw your performance at the rodeo yesterday," Rod said to Derek. "It was very good."

"Just something for me to pass the time before my gang meets-up and we go on the warpath again," Derek said.

"What's it like to be an outlaw?" Rod asked Derek.

"You can't explain it," Derek said. "It's something you've got to experience. And I've experienced many things. There is nothing like being an outlaw. Being an outlaw is on a whole other level than anything else. It has fulfilled me, and I want to continue to be fulfilled for the rest of my life. Tell me something, kid; have you ever rode a horse just to ride one?"

"Well, no," Rod said. "I mostly just take them into the pastures to graze, and I use them to drive the cattle."

"Cattle-driving is fine," Derek said, "grazing just sounds dead-boring."

Rod laughed.

"But, you've got to ride a horse as fast as you can on an open field that seems like it never ends with the wind blowing by you and your nerves releasing all the troubles that keep them in knots for no other reason just to do it."

"Now that you mention it, my nerves are usually pretty knotted," Rod said. "Maintaining the farm is tough stuff. Now, I have to worry about my pa's health."

"Don't tell me," Derek said. "You don't have the money to pay the doctor's bills?"

"Well, we could if we weren't being squeezed-dry by the bank and the governor."

"Hmmm…." Derek thought. "Aside from riding for no reason, there's nothing I like more about being an outlaw than sticking it to the governor. My gang leaves in a month and a half. What do you say I meet with you right here in this bar the night before the day we leave and we'll get you the money to fix your pa up nice and healthy and keep the farm owned by your family?"

"I would like to," Rod said, "but what do I tell my family? My pa thinks that the government should do whatever it wants."

"Tell 'em you're going to be working in a mine," Derek suggested. "It's believable, they'll appreciate it, and the money miners make isn't half-bad."

"Okay," Rod said. "I'm gonna do it. I'm gonna ride with you."

"In a month and a half from now, right here," Derek said, shaking Rod's hand. "What's your name, kid?"

"Rod McGillis," Rod said.

"That's a terrific cowboy name," Derek said. "Good to meet you, Rod."

"Good to ride with you, Derek," Rod said. "Thanks for just accepting me like that."

"Well, if you want to get an actual job where you get a weekly check with taxes withheld or you want a state government job you got to know somebody and it's just not fair...."

A big hand clamped down on Derek's shoulder and Derek turned around. It was a huge muscle for the sheriff's department, and a bunch of other deputies were in there. Their presence immediately killed all the fun they were having in the bar.

"You come with us so you can be hanged," one of the deputies said to Derek. "Make it nice and easy on yourself."

"What if I want it mean and hard on me?" Derek said.

"Take it up with him," one of the deputies said, pointing at the guy with the grip on Derek's shoulder.

"Okay, tiny," Derek said, "let's do this."

The big guy lifted Derek up in the air, spun around and launched him across the bar.

"Yahoo!" Derek shouted as he flew through the air and crashed onto a table. The people playing poker on the table were mad at the deputies for ruining their game, and everyone else was mad that they were there at all, so a huge brawl started.

Rod tried to stay out of it as best he could. He tried to watch Derek in the brawl. Derek was a great brawler. He was really scrappy and tough. He wasn't afraid to go against anyone. He was also good at being wary of sucker-punches, being cornered and other problems associated with free-for-alls.

But, when Derek went against the huge deputy, that's when the real cool stuff for Rod to watch started. Derek was like spider-monkey, leaping through the air, springing off of stuff, and moving at top-notch speed as he fought the deputy. The big, slow deputy couldn't keep up with Derek's moves and acrobatics, so he took a lot of punches from him. The other good thing about Derek leaping through the air for punches was that he would put all his bodyweight and force behind a punch. He only fought like that when he was facing-off with someone much bigger than him, though. If it was someone his size-range, he would fight normally.

Once all the deputies were taken out, Derek went over to Rod.

"I'm looking forward to causing some havoc with you, Rod," Derek said, shaking his hand.

"Likewise," Rod said.

"One more thing," Derek aid, walking to the door and stopping. "We're gonna need to get you a hat. Stay rebellious, everybody!"

Derek left the bar and went to find a hideout as best as he could.

"Help me!" a guy yelled, stuck under the big unconscious deputy.

The next day, Rod tried to explain to his family that he was going to go "work in a mine." True to what he thought, Sally and Molly were totally against it. Sally didn't want Rod to work in a mine where there were so many dangers and health risks, besides the chance of being stuck in a cave-in. Sally did not want Rod to end up like Stanley, health-wise.

Molly also didn't like the idea of Rod volunteering his health just for money. He also didn't want him to leave the family for three months at a time where she couldn't see him or talk to him for so long.

The only person that was in favor of Rod going to "work in a mine", just as Rod suspected, was Stanley. Stanley always supported men going to do dangerous things to take care of their family because he thought it made them even more of a man. Stanley assumed that everything he had taught Rod was working. So, if Stanley liked the idea, it had to happen. Rod was going to "work in the mine."

Rod Joins the Gang

The night that Rod was going to "catch the train to go to the mine", Molly wouldn't stop hugging him as he was getting ready to go.

"Molly, you're going to have to let go of me at some point," Rod said, getting his knapsack together.

"No," Molly argued. "If you actually leave, you're taking me all the way into the mine with you."

"I'm not taking my baby sister into the mine with me," Rod said, putting his bowie knife on him.

"Oh, then I guess you have to stay behind with us," Molly said.

"Molly," Sally said, walking into their room, "can't you just say 'good-bye' to your brother?"

"No," Molly said. "I'm not saying 'good-bye' because he's not leaving."

Sally wrenched Molly off of Rod. Rod finished packing and turned to Sally. She broke-down crying and hugged him even tighter than Molly did.

"We're going to miss you, Rod," Sally said, crying on him. "Thank you for doing this."

"I said I would do anything, ma," Rod said. "This is the payoff."

"Come on, let's let the boy go," Stanley grunted, walking into Rod and Molly's room.

Sally let go of Rod and Stanley approached him. Stanley stuck his hand out for Rod to shake. Sally rolled her eyes behind Stanley; Rod was going to do some serious work to help the family, she thought, and all Stanley did was shake his hand.

"It's mighty fine of you to do this for us, Rod," Stanley said, shaking his hand.

"A lot of it is for you, pa," Rod said.

"Well, all I can say is that you're going to be doing a lot of hard work, you might as well try to enjoy it."

"I sure will, pa."

"Sunny wants to say 'good-bye', Rod," Molly said, bringing the dog into their room.

Sunny jumped up at Rod and started to lick his face.

"I'm gonna miss you, buddy," Rod said, petting Sunny's head.

"You're gonna see some real dogs at the mine," Stanley said. "Actual guard dogs that chase away criminals and beasts."

When Rod left the house with his knapsack and they wouldn't let Sunny out with him, he started to whimper.

"None of the real dogs whine like that," Stanley criticized. "Rod's going to be around some dogs so tough that they could eat him whole."

Sally ran away crying. Molly stayed with Stanley and watched, through the window, Rod get on the last living horse they had and go toward "the train station."

The hardest thing for Rod was lying to Sally and Molly. It didn't bother him so much that he was lying to Stanley and disobeying all his teachings about being a citizen, because Stanley was going to let his beliefs kill him. All Sally and Molly wanted was the family to be together and safe. Rod was leaving to go throw himself into life-threatening danger where he could drop-down dead at any point. Rod also didn't appreciate Stanley's handshake too much. He was going to risk his life to get the money to repair Stanley, legally or not, and Stanley still couldn't bring himself to hug his son.

Rod got to the bar just as they were closing-up shop. He found Derek sitting at the counter having himself a drink before they left.

"You got a gun with you?" Derek asked Rod.

Rod moved one jacket side to show Derek he had a revolver.

"I also have a Winchester in my knapsack, and a bowie knife," Rod reported.

"That's a good arsenal," Derek said, finishing up his drink. He stood up and put a smile on.

"Now that we've got business taken care of, let's go have some fun."

Rod and Derek walked outside to their horses. They got on.

"How did your family take to the mine story?" Derek asked as their horses started to trot.

"They bought into it so much that my mother and sister was crying because I left," Rod said.

"That sounds like a good family to me," Derek said. "You be glad you've got them, Rod."

"I am" Rod said.

"Good," Derek said. "Hey, this speed is just not doing it for me. Let's kick some dust up."

Derek gave his horse a few kicks and Rod did the same. Their horses started to gallop. Rod had never ridden that fast for that long before.

Rod already liked Derek. Derek's personal charm was working already. Most of the time, Derek's charm worked instantaneously. People usually decided if they liked him or not at the first impression. Derck never worried about first impressions because he always acted the same way, even when he was drunk.

Derek and Rod made their way into the forest and out of the city. Riding through the forest was extremely difficult for Rod. He was constantly getting hit in the face by branches and leaves. It was also really hard to stay on the horse while it was riding so fast and on rough terrain. Derek seemed to have no problem with it. Rod assumed he had been riding forever and was used to anything. That was the truth.

Derek was so used to riding, that he didn't miss a step when they started getting chased by deputies on horses. Derek let go of the horse's reigns with both hands and took out both of his guns. He shot a deputy with each gun.

Rod didn't know what to do when a deputy rode alongside him. Derek rammed his horse into the deputy's horse and sent the deputy flying off the horse.

"Thanks," Rod said to Derek.

"Hey, anytime," Derek shouted.

Rod and Derek rode for a little while longer until they got far out of the city. That's when Rod noticed Derek's guitar.

"You play guitar?" Rod asked.

"Only when I'm not singing, playing the piano or the fiddle," Derek said.

Rod had never listened to very much music in his life, and always wondered what it was like to be able to play an instrument, much less multiple ones.

Rod and Derek rode up to a big mass of men on horseback. The ones that stood out the most to Rod were Tex because he was huge, Otis because he was the only black man, Villegas because of his crazy hair, and Marcus because he was young like him.

"Just sit tight with everybody else," Derek said to Rod.

Derek didn't seem like an outlaw in the sense that the governor and sheriff wanted people to think of outlaws. Derek seemed like a very down-to-earth, decent guy. Derek could have told Rod to do anything and he would have trusted him.

Derek went over to Tom. Tom already found something to complain about.

"We're not running a business where we take care of kids, Derek," Tom said. "I didn't complain when you brought Marcus in because he had absolutely nothing in his life. Who the hell is that?"

"Hey, good to see you," Derek said, trying to change the subject. "How's the family? I haven't seen you in a month and a half, Tom, lighten up!"

"You…. Get it together," Tom responded.

"Do I look like a guy who's not together?" Derek asked.

"You look like a guy that thinks he's invincible, and that's no good," Tom said.

"Aren't you ever going to invite me back to your place to see how pretty your daughter's gotten?" Derek asked. "Or did she wind up looking like you? Even worse, does she act like you?"

"I don't know what to say," Tom said. "We're not a big, jolly bunch of guys that have no requirements for admission in our gang, Derek."

"The last time I checked," Derek said, "I'm the boss, and anyone who wants to make money can join us. We're also not a rigid group that's hell-bent on following procedure. There'd have to be many more of you."

"I think I've made my point," Tom said. "Can we get this show on the road because it's getting late and the sheriff's deputies might come by and patrol this area and I notice that there are an increasing number of mosquitoes in the area and we don't need anybody getting all covered in bug-bites, you understand?"

"I understand something," Derek said.

Derek turned his horse so he faced the rest of the gang.

"Alright, I'm excited for another three months of fun, ain't ya'll?" Derek shouted.

Everyone cheered; Tex was the loudest.

"No, no," Tom said, cutting of the happiness. "This is not supposed to be fun. We're all strapped financially and we need to get down to business and execute properly and..."

Derek smacked Tom in the mouth to shut him up. Everyone laughed.

"I'm glad that everyone that's been with us has returned for another helping," Derek added, "and we all welcome the newcomers. Don't worry, fresh meat, there are no beatings to be a part of this gang, just trial by fire. Keep up with everybody else. There are two rules: take as much as you can, that's all you get for yourself, and follow me! Let's ride!"

"Yeeeeee-haaaaaaaa!" Tex shouted as everyone's horses kicked into a gallop.

"Vamanos!" Villegas yelled.

Rod wound-up riding next to Marcus.

"Hey, I'm Marcus," he said, introducing himself to Rod.

"I'm Rod," Rod said, shaking his hand.

"What brought you with us?"

"My family may lose the farm and my pop needs money to pay some important medical costs," Rod explained.

"You'll have no problem taking care of all that once we're done at the end of three months," Marcus said.

"You guys are good?"

"We're the best," Marcus said. "That's why you never hear about any other outlaw-gangs. They don't do nearly as much damage as we do."

Up at the front of the gang, Tom was still arguing with Derek.

"I still can't believe you brought another kid along," Tom said. "I don't even like too many new men joining us."

"So it's not morally offensive to you for kids to be outlaws," Derek said.

"They screw-up plans, they hold us back, there are all sorts of things that can go wrong," Tom said.

"Go meet the kid," Derek said. "He's been running his family's farm for some time and he's looking for money to save said farm and pay his sick father's medical bills. He's going to be at the top of his game here."

"I'll be the judge of that," Tom said, turning his horse around.

Tom let Derek catch up with him and rode alongside of him.

"I'm Tom," Tom said, shaking Rod's hand.

"I'm Rod," Rod said.

"Have you ridden a horse before?" Tom asked Rod.

"Not like this," Rod said.

"Yeah, it can be tricky at first."

The gang rode into a clearing and stopped.

"This looks like a good spot," Derek said, facing the gang and getting him off the horse.

"This is a good spot because it's close to the nearest town that we haven't robbed yet," Tom corrected.

"Yeah, let's go with that," Derek said, taking his guitar out and starting to play.

"Derek's playing," Marcus said to Rod. "You're not going to want to miss that."

Everyone got off their horses and sat down on the ground in front of Derek. Rod immediately noticed the ritualistic elements of Derek's concerts. He was a real performer, which Rod picked up on at the rodeo. Derek jumped, leapt and kicked in the air as he played. It was more than just listening to Derek's music.

The next day, Derek and Tom were scoping out the next town from the treetops.

"What do you think?" Derek asked, looking at the town through a scope.

"I think that we've never ran into this much security before," Tom said, looking through his scope at the town, which was filled with patrolling sheriff deputies.

"I meant about Rod," Derek said.

"Who's Rod?" Tom asked. "It's not the kid, is it?"

"Well, I like him," Derek said.

"You're thinking about how the new kid's a good guy while we're looking at around fifty deputies down there," Tom said. "It's interesting to see what your priorities are."

"Okay, let's talk about something you want to talk about," Derek said. "Do you have a plan?"

"That's more like it," Tom said. "As a matter of fact, I have a plan and it's a little something like…."

"That sounds great," Derek said, patting Tom on the shoulder and climbing down the tree.

"Are you serious?" Tom asked. "Why ask me if you don't even care?"

"I cared if you had a plan," Derek said. "I just didn't care what the plan was."

Derek and Tom walked back to the camp. Tom expected Derek to give everyone a quick discussion about the town, but he didn't, of course. Derek went right over to his horse, laid back on his knapsack and started playing a harmonica.

"You look like you have something to tell us, Tommy-Johnny," Tex said, looking up from a poker game between him, Otis and Villegas.

"Yes, everybody listen up," Tom said. "And quit it with the harmonica, Derek!'

Derek stopped playing his harmonica.

"Thank you," Tom said. "Now, we've got a little problem ahead of us. This town has got a little militia of deputies waiting for us. I assume it's us they're worried about. I think that we should…."

"And that's where you go wrong every time," Derek said, getting up and interrupting Tom.

"Guys," Derek said, "how's about we just ride up in that town with guns a-blazin' and just see what happens? The bank vault will eventually open itself up for us."

"I like it!" Tex shouted.

"Yeah," everybody else agreed.

"What do you think, Tom?" Derek asked.

"Does it even matter?" Tom asked.

The whole gang laughed.

"That settles it," Tom said. "At dawn, we…"

"Who said anything about dawn?" Derek argued. "Let's let the sun get a little overhead before we do anything. Guys, how about it?"

"Good idea! Tex yelled.

Derek and Tom got out of their spotlights for the day.

"Marcus, new guy," Otis said, waving them over to the poker game. "Get in on this."

Rod and Marcus walked over to the three men and sat down.

"Ever played poker before?" Villegas asked Rod.

"No, never," Rod said.

"That's fine," Tex said. "Derek's not playing, so no one's gonna lose big-time."

"Did someone invite me to play poker?" Derek shouted. He and Tom were sitting over by their horses.

"No, no one wants you to play with us!" Otis shouted.

For the rest of the day, they all played cards. Rod got the hang of it pretty fast and won a few rounds.

Sleeping out in the open was hard for Rod to get used to. He had never been outside while wolves were howling in the woods, and he heard sounds from animals he'd never heard before. He didn't like sleeping on the outside ground; he started to question how much of an outdoorsman he really was. The ground was hard and uncomfortable and the grass made his skin itchy. It also got really cold at night, and he wasn't used t that being inside his house. Rod was starting to figure out why Stanley turned out the way he did.

The next morning, Rod woke up with severe back pain. Every time he moved any part of his body, his bones started to crack and his muscles were really tight.

"Don't tell me," Derek said, walking over to him. "First night sleeping outside?"

"You've got it," Rod said, cracking his own back and wincing.

"You get used to it," Marcus said.

"Excuse me, Derek," Tom said, walking up and interrupting. "We're late as it is. Could we get moving?"

"Good morning," Derek said to Tom. "It looks like it's gonna be a good day, aren't you excited about that? Why does everything have to be rushed with you?"

"Oh, I'm sorry," Tom said. "I didn't think to take the time to smell the flowers while the state militia is circling where we slept."

"Well, let's take the time to smell some flowers together," Derek said, picking a flower out of the ground and sniffing it. Marcus was laughing at how much Derek was bothering Tom, but Rod didn't feel like he was part of the group enough just yet to laugh. It was amusing, though.

"What is this, lilac?" Derek asked. "I could sit down all day smelling this. I just got a good idea, Tommy. Why don't you bring this one back for the wife? I'll try and pin it on you."

Derek went to try and put the flower in one of Tom's pockets. Tom smacked it out of Derek's hand.

"The deputies aren't going to smell flowers with you," Tom said. "They're going to kill you. Let's go now."

"Let's see," Derek said. "Boys, whose ready?"

"Hold it a moment, boss," Tex said. He lifted his leg and released a fart that the wind took toward Surge. Surge's facial muscles started to contort and he tried to wave the foul air out of his way.

"Holy hell, that's awful!" Otis shouted, getting on his horse and wrapping a bandana in front of his face.

"Really, Tex?" Villegas asked, riding off toward the town.

"Wait, what about the plan?" Tom shouted, getting on his horse. "Can't we... Tex, what the hell did you eat?"

Rod could feel the rush to get away from Tex's stench. It was the worst thing he had ever smelled. The last thing he wanted to do was to remain in the vicinity of the stench, even though he was about to ride into a life-threatening fight. Rod got on his horse and caught up with everyone else.

Tex thought he was the last person left at the camp, and he was chuckling as he casually got on his horse. He was about to ride off, but he saw Marcus passed-out on the ground. The smell was too much for him.

"Whoa, Mark," Tex said, getting off his horse and walking over to Marcus. Tex was still laughing.

"Come on, boy," Tex said, slapping Marcus' face. "I know it wasn't that bad."

Tex stopped laughing when it crossed his mind that it may have killed him.

"Well, if worse comes to worse," Tex said to himself, "at least Tom will be glad I got everybody rolling."

Against Tom's angry shouts, Derek felt like it would be fun to ride into the town on the path of highest visibility. The deputies saw them from a mile away.

"Here they come!" a deputy yelled, running to the front of the town's main street.

"Everyone get ready to fire!" the local sheriff yelled. "Hold it, where's the rest of them...."

There was only a third of Derek's gang riding straight into the town. The second third rode into the town from the right alleyways and mowed-over the deputies from one side. The deputies that managed to get out of the way tried to run down the other end of the main street. The last third of Derek's gang rode in from the back of the town and started gunning down the deputies on the main street.

"Yeah, scatter!" Villegas shouted, shooting into a trio of deputies with a shotgun.

The gang had to get off all their horses when the deputies on the rooftops started firing on them. Luckily, the outlaws had trained their horses to flee the scene when that happened, so they never lost their horses. Even Rod's horse figured out that he needed to follow the other horses and got away.

Rod really didn't know what to do. He realized that he couldn't possibly kill an actual person, and he didn't want to be shot in the out-of-control crossfire.

So, Rod darted into the nearest building and ran through the door. He turned around, pulled out his gun and opened the door to a crack. Someone pulled the door shut from the inside and shoved Rod face-first into the door. Rod turned around and the only reason he missed taking a knife in the forehead was because the drunken deputy missed him. Rod kicked the deputy in the groin and tried to pick up his revolver, which he had dropped. The deputy pulled out another knife and slashed Rod's hand as he reached for his gun. The deputy tried to slash at Rod's arm, but Rod had backed up and got out of the way.

The deputy lunged at Rod and tried to cut his shoulder. Rod dashed to the side and let the deputy throw himself right into the wall. While he was dazed, Rod pulled his back by his shirt and let the deputy trip over his shirt. Rod pinned the deputy down and delivered a few punches to his face while he was down. The deputy somehow had another knife, which he tried to slash Rod in the face with. Rod just barely rolled out of the way.

The deputy struggled to get up, and Rod got low and drove him into the bar counter, this breaking the deputy's spine. The deputy slumped down to his behind on the floor and started playing with his knife.

Rod went over to his revolver, picked it up, and without even thinking, shot the deputy in the forehead. It didn't bother Rod too much because that deputy outright tried to kill him three times, and the deputy seemed like a wild animal with respect to his mind and intelligence, so Rod was okay with it.

Rod opened the door and walked outside, a lot more energized at having won a fight with a member of the Wyoming sheriff's department. His confidence was immediately crushed by the tidal-wave of reality that was the battle in the town.

Rod dove behind a barrel to avoid a few bullets that tore-up where he had been standing.

"Hey, Rod!" Derek shouted, hiding behind a barrel in the next building over. "Come on to the roof with me!"

Rod was about to shout that a deputy had just stepped behind Derek and was about to shoot him in the head, but Derek aimed a gun behind him and shot the deputy without looking.

"Come on, now!" Derek yelled, getting ready to use his double-guns. "I'll give you some cover fire!"

Rod stood up and sprinted across the way toward the porch where Derek was. The whole time Rod was running, Derek was giving him cover fire, just as he promised.

Rod made it over there and he and Derek made their way up to the rooftop, where they had the jump on the sharp-shooter deputies. Derek, with one gun, took out each one of them with a bullet right in the neck.

"That was really good," Rod said, amazed.

"That wasn't nothing," Derek said. "You want to see something really impressive?"

Derek had Rod join him right at the edge of the rooftop. Derek took both guns out and hit each of the deputies that were on all the rooftops. There were some huge distances for Derek to handle.

"That was really, really good," Rod said.

"Aw, shucks," Derek said. "I'm sure we'll have you shooting like that in good time."

Rod couldn't believe he would ever be able to shoot like that in his life, even in great time.

"Tom, how are we doing down there?" Derek shouted down to Tom.

"We've got the streets and alleys secured!" Tom shouted. "They're still occupying the bank!"

"Which building is it?" Derek asked.

"All the way down at the end of your row!" Tom yelled.

"Alright," Derek said, backing up to the opposite end of the rooftop, "are you a jumper, Rod?"

"Huh?" Rod asked.

Derek got a running start and leapt onto the other rooftop.

"I won't wait up for you!" Derek shouted back.

Rod had to try it. He was still exhilarated from fighting the deputy in the bar. Rod got a good running start for himself and he actually made it.

"Ha, ha!" Derek yelled. "Well done!"

Rod had never met anyone that enjoyed what they did more than Derek. Stanley did like being a hard-working farmer, but he didn't let it show the way Derek did. Derek seemed happy-as-can-be while he was outlawing.

Rod and Derek hopped from rooftop to rooftop until they got to the bank's rooftop. There was a trapdoor on the roof and Derek carefully opened it. He could see sheriff deputies shooting out of the bank from the inside.

"Good thing I keep this handy," Derek said, taking out a lasso from his jacket.

"What's that gonna do?" Rod asked.

Derek wrapped one end around himself and secured the other end to the handle of the trapdoor.

"Are you sure that will hold you?" Rod asked.

"That would ruin the spontaneity of the whole thing, kid," Derek said, grinning. Don't wait up."

Derek dropped himself into the bank through the roof and brought out his double-revolvers. The lasso's rope was spinning and he took-out every deputy in the room as he twirled in mid-air.

"Untie me!" Derek called up to Rod.

Rod untied the lasso and Derek softly landed on the floor of the bank.

"That was terrific!" Rod shouted down.

"Just a little something-something," Derek said, putting the lasso away.

Rod left the rooftop and made his way down into the bank. He got there to find Derek, Tom and Otis trying to break the vault door with a pole.

"Has anyone seen Tex?" Tom shouted. "We could really use him here!"

"He's here," Marcus said, walking into the bank with Tex.

"Nice of you to join us," Tom said, angrily. "What the hell happened?"

"Tom, he passed-out because of my stench," Tex defended.

"Oh," Tom said. "Well, why don't you open this door to make up for that wretched smell?"

Tex took the metal pole from Derek and bashed the vault's door in.

"That should do it," Tex said, putting the pole down.

Derek and Tom ripped the door out and tossed it aside.

"Alright, let's clean-up," Derek said, opening up a sack and starting to put all the money into it. "Tom, where's the closest town to here?"

"Why?" Tom asked, helping load-up the money.

"Because I want all of Roth's money to turn into hooker-tips," Derek said.

"You need to learn how to be responsible, you know," Tom said to Derek.

"Here we go," Otis said.

"You can't just throw your money at prostitutes and bar-tenders for the rest of your life," Tom preached. "You need to start planning ahead."

"No, you need to plan ahead," Derek said. "I don't. You have a wife and daughter you need to take care, and I don't. And that's okay."

"Why don't you put your money in the bank?" Tom asked. "They'll pay you money for having it there."

"Tom, we're bank robbers," Derek said. "You're telling a bank robber to put his money in the bank?"

"I'm not gonna tell you anything anymore," Tom said.

"We both know that's not gonna happen," Derek said, patting Tom's shoulder. "Now, let's all go to the next town and have some fun, we're done with this work."

"If you'd follow my carefully-scripted plans, it would be work," Tom complained. "It's almost like this is all a big game to you."

"Hey, you're finally catching on," Derek said, leaving the vault. "I was hoping I was laying it on pretty thick."

"Don't worry about that," Tom said, following Derek out. "I had no problem figuring out you thought our work was just something to pass the time for you."

"Let's go, guys!" Derek shouted to the rest of the gang.

Everyone in the gang got together and they went to find their horses. Along the way, Rod checked his pockets to check how much he took for himself. He only grabbed two small stacks of bills. Considering all the big-boys in the gang (Derek, Tom, Tex, Otis, Villegas) all had huge sacks of money, Rod thought that he kind of missed out. But, Rod had as much money in his pocket as half the farm as worth. That was a terrific start.

"Maim" Street

There was only one town with a street that was actually called Main Street in Wyoming. It was official; every map had the street listed as Main Street.

But there was a twist. The governor, the sheriff and all his deputies referred to it as "Maim Street." The reason for that was the town that it was located in turned out to be the biggest outlaw-town in the entire state. This was a direct result of Nolan's actions. All the people that were hit by his ill-advised economic policies flocked there. They were originally a mixture of cowboy-gangs, but they quickly saw the benefit of them combining forces and inhabiting the town in complete defiance of the governor and sheriff. The governor and everyone close to him called the whole town "Maim Street" because the town was maimed by the low-life culture of being an outlaw and being poor. If a moderate rich person in Wyoming ever started to feel compassion for the people struggling in Wyoming, he would remind them what "Maim Street" was like, and it immediately made them feel good and proud to be rich.

Naturally, the people of "Maim Street" were big fans of Derek. The town became his top hideout in the entire state, just above only a few other places he liked to lay low. He was always welcome in "Maim Street" for as long as he and his gang liked to stay. They always got to stay in any room in any building for free to eat and drink whatever they wanted, also for free. Hey went there all the time, but the governor and sheriff never knew, and they went there even more than Derek did.

The governor and sheriff loved to periodically take trips to "Maim Street" and verbally abuse the entire town and the entire population. They were always accompanied by heavily-armed security, of course, not like it made a difference. The people of "Maim Street" turned into such habitual drunks and deadbeats that they lost their ability to fight back and keep up with the outlaw lifestyle. So much of their brain was inactive from all the drinking that a lot of them didn't even realize that they were being insulted when the governor and sheriff arrived.

There were a few people that were able to keep their wits about them, and there was only one person that actually didn't like Derek. That person was Jessica, but everyone called her "Jess."

Jess used to be Derek's only serious girlfriend and it got so serious that they were set to actually get married. Derek realized that he wasn't the settle-down type of guy, and even less of a one-woman guy. Derek bailed on her and went to a hooker-bar instead of going to the chapel. Ever since then, they were not good friends. But, she didn't hold that against the rest of the gang.

All of Wyoming had the idea that Derek had a high standard for women that he fooled-around with, but everyone in the gang agreed that Jess was better than all of them. Tom knew that Derek internally hated himself for letting her go, and figured that Derek should talk about it to be at peace with himself. But, Derek was too proud to admit to anything like that, and the only emotion he liked to let out was joy.

It was true that Jess was the best girl that Derek ever had. She was much smarter than him and even smarter than the people that worked in the governor's cabinet. That was good for Derek; Jess got him to clean up his act much better than Tom could ever dream to. She was also much more attractive than any other girl Derek had been with. She was tall, she wasn't muscular but she projected a lot of strength about her, and she had long, brown hair which was Derek's favorite.

The governor and sheriff decided to make a trip to "Maim Street" that day. They walked in there with at least fifty deputies behind them, ready to start shooting the town at the drop of a hat.

Nolan and Ralph stopped at the beginning of the actual main street of the town and looked around. The streets, alleys and rooms were filled with people that were passed-out drunk or people fighting. The random fights always started over nothing and they had a snowball-effect, picking up more participants as the fights moved throughout the town.

Not a single window didn't have a crack in it and not a single door was perfectly on its hinges. Not a single building had rotting and termite-ridden walls, and not a single roof wasn't semi-caved-in. It was a real crappy town.

"Look at this shit-hole, Ralph," Nolan said, grinning at the town.

"I've pissed in better places than this," Ralph remarked. "Keep a lookout, boys." The deputies were all on their toes for anything that could happen.

Nolan and Ralph walked into a bar and went up to the counter. Everyone was glaring at them and giving them cross looks.

"What's the most expensive thing you've got to drink in these parts?" Nolan asked, trying not to laugh. Ralph did allow himself to laugh.

"Just some beer that we brewed ourselves out back," the bar-tender said, not appreciating being offended. "Nothing like the imported European stuff you're used to."

"I had a feeling," Nolan said.

In her room above the bar, Jess opened the door to walk downstairs. A young boy with his skin tanned from always being covered in mud and dirt stopped her.

"You can't go down there, Jess," the boy warned her. "The governor and sheriff are here."

"They're downstairs, Billy?" Jess whispered to him.

Billy nodded with his eyes wide with fear.

"Okay, thanks for telling me," Jess said.

"Please go back in your room and don't come out until they're gone, Jess," the boy pleaded.

"I promise," Jess said, rubbing his hair. "I'll call on you if they give me any trouble, okay?

"Okay, Miss Jess," Billy said.

Jess waited until Billy walked away and she peered down into the bar to get a good look at the governor and the sheriff. She didn't like what she was seeing. Ralph had a few of his deputies holding people-up while he and Nolan took money from whoever they wanted.

Jess wanted to keep her promise to Billy and went back in her room to avoid being seen by the governor or sheriff.

Everyone in "Maim Street" was very protective of Jess because of her involvement with Derek. Luckily for her, Nolan and Ralph never knew of her former engagement to Derek, or that they even knew each other. But, "Maim Street" wanted to do everything to protect Jess from being used by Nolan against Derek. And Nolan would use anyone against Derek; he wouldn't let up if his bait was a woman or a kid. Everyone was in danger.

The next town over from the one that the gang had just robbed didn't have any bank, any post office, or anything that was associated with big money or government. That was where the gang decided to take the night off and decompress. Tom was the big reason that they needed to relax.

The next morning, Tom went around the town to wake everyone up and get them ready to ride. Everybody was extremely hung-over and not in the mood to ride.

Rod didn't think that anyone was feeling it as bad as he was. His headache was blinding him, his limbs felt useless and floppy, and his vision was blurry. He already wished he utilized one of his father's lessons: don't drink too much at once.

Rod's vision started to come back when he saw Tom enter the room.

"Is that you, Tom?" Rod asked.

"Yep," Tom said. "Have you seen Derek?"

"Nope," Rod said. 'Hey, Tom, how did Derek get that scar on his face?"

"I don't know," Tom said. "Nobody knows. He had it when I first met him."

Tom left the room to go look for Derek. Rod sat down back down on the floor. A becoming prostitute that was just a little older than him rolled over and her arm laid across his lap.

"Oh, yeah," Rod said. "I remember what happened last night."

"First time waking up after drinking all night?" Marcus asked, sitting up and rubbing his eyes.

"Yep," Rod said, moving the girl off of him and standing up. "How much do you know about Derek?"

"I don't know anything about his family or his childhood," Marcus said. "He had a serious girlfriend at one point..."

"Derek?" Rod asked, laughing. "Serious girlfriend?"

"Yeah, we all thought it was funny when he first told us," Marcus said. "But, he was able to completely destroy his relationship with her thereafter. I know he's good friends with some Apache tribe; we go to their territory all the time. There's another outlaw that hates Derek, he's Bolton Butler. That's that."

The girl that was asleep on Rod got up and wrapped her arms around his neck.

"How much more money do you got?" she asked.

"Not enough to throw around," Rod said.

"Oh," the girl said. "Well, good-bye."

The girl left the room.

"Are they all that charming?" Rod asked Marcus.

"I've never heard one of them talk," Marcus said.

Rod and Marcus went outside and met with the rest of the gang.

"Alright, guys," Tom said to everyone. "We didn't expect this many deputies to be in our path. So, we're going to go to Maim Street until the heat cools off. How does that sound to everybody?"

"Sounds like a whole week of nights like the one we just had," Surge said.

"Hey, I am in," Tex said.

"Muy bueno," Villegas agreed.

"How about you, big-shot?" Tom asked Derek.

"You know," Derek said, with humorous reserve, "I've been hearing some pretty negatory stuff about the weather out by Maim Street. A lot of cold, bitter air that just can't get over how the warm front has passed by...."

"That's tough crap," Tom said. "We're going to Maim Street!"

"You're gonna like Maim Street, for sure," Marcus said to Rod. "Every second is like the night we all just had, but you don't wake up all groggy."

"Not groggy?" Rod asked. "Beautiful."

It was very depressing at the McGillis farm without Rod there. Food was really scarce and on short supply because Rod wasn't able to do any hunting and Stanley was asleep throughout all hours of the day. Sally and Molly unsuccessfully tried their hand at farming. It was really tough work for them and they got out less than what they put in. It didn't help that they really missed Rod, and that was affecting their mood.

After Sally and Molly finished as much work as they could do for the day, Molly just sat around on the front porch, glumly petting Sunny. Sunny wasn't as happy without Rod, either.

Sally walked out onto the porch and sat next to Molly.

"You miss him, don't you?" Sally asked Molly.

"Yeah," Molly sighed. "I miss him, and I'm afraid that he's hurt or something in that mine."

"That's exactly why I didn't want him to leave," Sally said.

Every time Derek showed-up to "Maim Street," it was like he was a populist candidate for the House of Representatives whose main strength was being able to arise mass support.

The gang paraded into the town in the face of a hero's welcome. Every single person in "Maim Street" wished they were like Derek and idolized him. It was a blessing every visit he made to their home.

Derek, being a people-person, high-fived and shook hands with as many people as he could. They seemed to want him hear something from him, so he climbed up onto an awning and faced the entire town. Derek took a quick look for Jess, and saw her standing by herself, almost like she was moping around, at the door of the town's bar. She did find the time to see him in, though.

"Alright," Derek said, "ya'll want to hear some words of wisdom from me? Well, fyi, in the last month and a half I spent some time in Roth's...."

Derek was cut-off by angry boos and shouts from the crowd. The very mention of the governor's name pushed their buttons.

"I'm with you," Derek agreed, taking control of the crowd back. "I stood around as many wanted posters of myself as I could; saying 'howdy' to people and no one pointed me out to Hatcher's...."

More boos.

"I like the mindsets here," Derek said. "I even got the opportunity to break a rodeo record, which I did."

Derek got a big applause for that.

"My point is," Derek said, "we are becoming stronger among the normal people of Wyoming, the people that aren't millionaires."

More boos.

"Uh-huh," Derek said. "My other point is, do not feel the need to hide who you are. Do not be afraid to be a regular person, and don't let the governor and sheriff persecute for being who you are."

Derek hopped down from the awning and had a lot of hands to shake and slap. While he was satisfying all this, he looked for Jess again. She waited until he saw her sourpuss, turned around and went back up into her room in the bar.

Derek found young Billy in the crowd.

"Hey, little guy," Derek said, rubbing his head with his knuckles. "Listen, how has Jess been lately?"

"Same as usual," Billy said.

"Has she been saying anything about me?" Derek asked. "I won't tell her I heard it from you."

"She hasn't," Billy said. "She never wants to talk about you."

"Whoa," Derek said. "That scares me more than if she railed about me all the time. Thanks, little guy. Here's a little something for your troubles."

Derek flipped him a coin, and then he and his gang went into the bar as "Maim Street" went back to normal after getting over his presence. Derek saw Jess sitting with a couple of her friends at the bar. Her friends weren't like her; they continued to like Derek after the past because they didn't have nearly as much self-respect as she did.

"Tex, why don't you get on the piano and lighten the mood a bit?" Derek suggested. "Play one of those Texan foot-tappers."

"I got a terrific one ya'll will like," Tex said, walking over to the piano and starting-up a really loud, fast tune that would have gotten everybody swinging if the air wasn't so thick with tension.

Derek slowly walked over to the girls at the counter.

"Hi, Derek," all of Jess' friends said to him at once.

"Hello," Jess muttered, taking a shot of whiskey.

"Do you usually drink like this?" Derek asked Jess. "I like to drink to perk myself up. Ladies, do you agree?"

"Yeah, Derek," all of them said.

"I don't drink while I'm moping all over the place and spreading dread."

"Piss off, Derek," Jess muttered.

"Come on," Derek said to Jess. "Why don't we have sex? I'm sure that will lift your spirits."

"No," Jess said, drinking another shot of whiskey.

"I have some sugar to sweeten-up this deal," Derek said. "Why don't your friends join us? You may not even notice me."

"Oh, that sounds like fun," one of her friends said. The rest of the girls agreed.

"They're team-players, Jess," Derek said.

"Go away," Jess said, turning away from him on her barstool.

"How about just some heavy-duty foreplay?" Derek asked.

"You know what, Derek?" Jess asked, getting up and walking over to Tom. "Why don't I make out with Tom right here in front of you?"

Jess knocked Tom's hat off his head.

"I don't think that'll keep him from jumping in, Jess," Tom said.

"You and Tom?" Derek asked, laughing. "He'd pass the hell out!"

"No," Tom said, "he'll maturely extricate himself from the encounter because he has a wife and daughter and he's happy with that."

"Okay, thanks for helping, Tom," Jess said, picking his hat up and handing him his hat.

Jess saw Rod and went over to him.

"What if I banged your newest guy, Derek?" Jess asked, putting her arm around Rod. Rod didn't know what to do.

"Hey Rod, meet Jess," Derek said. "Jess, this is Rod. I took it upon myself to help him out with his family troubles."

"Ha!" Jess said. "Rod, he'll 'fix' your problems by giving you many more and you won't even remember what you wanted to take care of in the first place."

"Okay," Derek said, "if we're not gonna have a nice, friendly time together I'll leave."

"It took you long enough to figure out we weren't gonna have a nice time," Jess said.

"Well," Derek said, "if you're going to refuse to act like a normal person, I'll go find someone out the hundreds of people out there that worship me."

"Derek, cool it," Tom said.

Tex stopped playing.

"Honey, you're not punishing me, you're punishing yourself," Derek said, instantly dropping his easy-going nature and getting angry. Rod thought it was a completely different person.

"So, I don't need to be around while you wallow in your damn depression," Derek snapped.

Derek walked through the door of the bar and slammed the door shut. They heard him punch the door after it shut.

"I'll go try and get something out of him," Tom said, leaving the bar.

"Well, that was inevitable," Tex said, starting to play a blues song.

Rod noticed a tear in Jess' eye and she noticed that he was still there.

"Oh, sorry about that," Jess said, getting off of Rod. "Nice to meet you."

"Yeah, a pleasure," Rod said. "Except for.... You know.... Derek."

"Marcus, Rod," Jess said, "why don't you have a drink with us and get us caught-up on everything?"

Rod and Marcus sat with Jess and her friends at the bar counter while Tex continued to play the piano and Villegas started an upbeat Spanish rhythm.

Jess decided to cut herself off from her heavy liquor because Derek wasn't bothering her anymore, but she did cover the bill for Marcus and Rod's drinks.

"Have you been keeping yourself safe from our enemies, Jess?" Marcus asked her.

"I do my best," Jess said, "but sometimes I need by guard Billy to look out for me. The governor and sheriff gave us a visit just before you guys showed up."

"They come here?" Rod asked.

"All the time," one of Jess' friends said.

"I live right outside the capitol and he's always got everyone afraid of this place," Rod admitted. "But, it doesn't seem half bad."

"Take everything the governor and sheriff say and the opposite is reality," Jess said.

"I'm starting to figure that out."

"When was the last time you had a good time?" one of Jess' friends said, trying to get comfortable with Rod on his stool. Rod quickly figured out she was another prostitute.

"Leave him alone," Jess said to her. "He's obviously new to all this."

"Fine," the girl said. "We're going to go see if Derek's offer is still on the table."

They all got up and left.

"That offer is always available," Jess muttered. "It could be right in the middle of Tom's funeral and Derek would try to pick-up grieving girls. Sorry, I know you ride with him."

"Everybody needs to hear about their problems at some point," Rod said.

"What made you join the group?" Jess asked.

"My family might lose their farm and my pa needs money to take care of some serious medical operations," Rod explained.

"I'm so sorry," Jess said. "I should have kept my mouth shut."

"Don't worry about it," Rod reassured.

"They're okay with you being an outlaw to take care of everything?" Marcus asked.

"They think I'm working in a mine for the 3 months," Rod said. "Derek helped me come up with that one."

"Yeah, he's a terrific liar," Jess said. "But, the good news is that your situation is the kind that he's the most sympathetic to."

During the duration of the time they were hiding at "Maim Street", (they didn't think of it so much as hiding as partying), Rod learned about balancing being a normal person with being an outlaw. He talked to a lot of people there that started out just like him; they were completely desperate and out of options to take care of their families or farms that they turned to crime. But, they got so lost in their lifestyle that they turned into burnouts.

Rod did find that there were some people that were able to hang onto reality: Derek and his whole gang, Jess, Billy and a few others. Those were the people that Rod spent most of his time with. Although Billy was barely even Molly's age. Rod felt extremely bizarre about that. He could never imagine Molly being born right into the necessity of sleeping with men for money. That kind of thing made Rod wish he was at home.

Rod always loved being at his far with his family, but he never imagined that he would ever wish he was at home more than he did. But, after a while he saw the appeal of "Maim Street" under the literal maiming. Everyone that lived there was like one big family and everyone treated each other like they were very close relatives and friends. Rod noticed that one of the biggest forms of comradery was paying for someone else's drink. That seemed a bit shallow to him from what he was used to, but to them it was extremely appreciated.

When Derek and his gang showed up, it was like a holiday season in paradise. The people of "Maim Street never had any worries or responsibilities; they would just hunt or grow whenever they needed food and had great satisfaction in making their own beer. Other than that, they were totally care-free. But, when Derek and the guys came around town, the energy-levels increased and there was nonstop partying.

Rod was hearing some of the best music he'd ever heard in his life. Derek was constantly putting on shows for everybody at every instrument he could find. He had a small band behind him; Tom was solid at the bass, Villegas was a good back-up guitarist, Tex could make a good beat with percussion-style instruments, and Surge was pretty good with horn-type things.

Derek also brought a lot of good business for the bar-tenders and hookers in "Maim Street." In fact, that's all he usually spent his money on, except when he occasionally got his weapons furnished and tuned-up. He also made sure his horse was well-fed, but it was the people who gave him food, beer and sex that really got him spending. Derek also encouraged the rest of the gang to spend like that.

"There's nothing like helping working women," Derek would always say. He half-meant it as a joke. This kind of thing from Derek got Jess even more angry with Derek; she really wanted women to empower themselves in Wyoming and that didn't start with them being sex-objects. Nolan did a lot to keep women subjugated, too.

Nolan was a big image in "Maim Street," even more when Derek was around. There were posters of him in every single room in "Maim Street" that were draped over dartboards. They were old campaign posters, now they were targets. There were giant ragdolls of him that were used to light fires or to be hung from tree branches and people threw knives and shot at them. The people of "Maim Street" were very bitter about the governor. One comedy-writer in the town had a book out that was filled with jokes about the governor, and they were all somehow true.

The highlight of the time in "Maim Street" was when Derek conspired to get Tom really drunk, and it worked. Whenever they went out, Tom would only drink water. He didn't know that his water was getting mixed with whiskey. Tom would constantly remark at how the water "had a kick to it." Everybody would crack-up with laughter, and Tom would have no idea what was going on under his nose.

No one had ever seen Tom drunk before. They always tried to get him drunk before, but Tom was pretty clever and had caught on to every plan before, but he slipped-up this time around. And it cost him, big time. Tom went totally nuts and went even crazier than Derek did when he was drunk. That was the highest bar ever set on any standard. Tom had gotten on stage with a bunch of showgirls, dressed the part, and performed an entire dance routine with them. Derek hid his clothes while he was up there, and the next morning when everyone was aware and alert, Tom had to go through the entire town looking for his clothes in a tight skirt and bra. He wouldn't be allowed to forget about that for a long time.

Amidst all the craziness, Rod and Jess became really good friends. Rod quickly picked up on all the traits that Derek liked; strange that he liked them at all, and Jess thought that Rod was one of the only sensible people she'd ever met in addition to Tom, Marcus and Billy. Here was nothing Tom could criticize Jess about; she had everything together. Tom did take a lot of time to commend her for that and encourage her to keep it up. Even when Tom was positive, he could get annoying.

What Rod really liked about Jess was her relationship with Billy. Billy was an orphan from birth and Jess was like a mother to him. Rod could tell she was raising him right; Jess taught the boy how to read and write, Derek couldn't do any of that, and how to be a good person. Derek could have used a few lessons in that.

What Jess liked about Rod was how he had a family and that he was risking his own life in the most dangerous way to save his family from a disaster. Jess found herself wishing that she was a few years younger and Rod was a few years older so they could be together. She noticed that Rod wasn't bad-looking either.

Rod agreed with Jess and Tom's conclusions that Derek was a complete idiot for letting Jess get away for no reason.

The Apaches

In the pecking order of power in Wyoming, it was the governor, then the sheriff, followed by the rich, and then the old citizens, the working masses began the negative favor, then the Indians, and cowboys at the bottom.

Of course, every stratum that Nolan was hostile towards thought they had it the worst. The poor was dumbfounded that they did such hard work on Wyoming and got absolutely no compensation while Nolan poured tax cuts into the pockets of the rich and the sheriff's department, after he filled his own bank accounts. The cowboys, who usually just tried to live a life of free-riding in the wilderness, were furious that they were constantly being shot at for no reason by lawmen. And the Indians, who thought that it couldn't get any worse than Andrew Jackson, were now thinking that Nolan was the end of their people and culture.

Over the years, the Indians had been funneled up into that northwest corner of the states. Nolan only blamed the Indians for that. Nolan wasn't even a Southerner, but there was no one who believed in keeping non-whites at the bottom of the social order more than him. It's not like he even singled anybody out. The Chinese that worked on railroads and in mines, the blacks that tried to set-up something of a life after being freed from slavery, and the Indians that were trying as hard as they could to avoid extinction were under ruthless attack from the governor and sheriff.

It was a very rare day in the governor's mansion. Not the mansion that the governor owned on the side, but the actual state government mansion that was just as decadent as his own place. Nolan actually received a labor union boss as he had lunch with his top economic advisor and the sheriff in a dining hall that was something like a dining hall in an English and French castle.

The union boss, though he was actually granted a session with the governor, was being shown no respect. They wouldn't let him sit down; there were deputies in every corner of the room that were ready to shoot him right between the eyes if he even reached for one of Nolan's chairs with his dirty hands. They didn't offer him a drink or anything. Every single thing Nolan had in the mansion was worth more than this guy made in a year.

The boss didn't even want to unionize at first. He just wanted to work and make a decent living based on how hard he worked. But, he couldn't get that. Nolan removed nearly all regulations on employer treatment of workers in Wyoming. So, managers of businesses there were free to make their workers be on the job for as long as they wanted to schedule them, there were no rules on safety hazards and health concerns, and forget about sick leave. The boss finally had enough and wanted to try and work with the governor for some reasonable agreement. That was a long shot.

"Alright....guy," Nolan said. "What is it that you want?"

"My name is Jethro," the boss said.

"Trust me," Nolan said. "Guy is better."

Ralph tried to stop from spitting out his scotch as he laughed.

"It's like this," Jethro said. "We've got some complaints about the conditions we've been working under."

"Uh-huh," Nolan said, not really listening.

"People have been dying, governor," Jethro boomed.

"What kind of work do you do?" Nolan asked.

"I work on railroads," Jethro said. "People I work with get their fingers and hands taken off, guys never get to go home to their families, and a couple of workers are almost ninety-years-old. This can't go on."

"Really?" Nolan asked. "Because everything seems fine from where we are."

Jethro slammed his fist on the table. The deputies ran up to him and shoved their guns in his face. Ralph got up and positioned a knife on Jethro to cut his jugular. Nolan wiped his mouth with a napkin and got up.

"That's what I don't like about you laborers," Nolan said. "You can't act civilized."

"You're sitting here while hundreds of people are getting dismembered for nearly no pay," Jethro said, sweating. "And how about some security from the Indians?"

"Let me tell you something about the Indians," Nolan said. "They...."

"Governor," a deputy said, walking in with an Apache ambassador. "The savage is here."

"Not savage!" the Indian angrily shouted.

The guns went from Jethro to the Indian.

"Easy does it, chief," Ralph said.

"Now, I have a pretty good idea of what you're used to," Nolan said to the Indian. "But over here we live in a society where people act civilized to each other. Can you do that for me?"

The Indian hesitated because he was very insulted that the governor insinuated that he and his people weren't civilized and lived in a joke of a society. But, he had to be grateful that the governor even agreed to allow him inside the city boundaries.

"Yes," the Indian choked.

"That's weird," Nolan said. "I don't see any of your.... Oh, let's call them people. I'm trying to figure out who you're talking to."

"Yes, sir," the Indian said, gulping and swallowing his pride.

"That's better," Nolan said. "Everybody back up and let's try to keep this friendly."

The deputies still kept their barrels up, but backed up to their corners.

"Indian, this labor union leader has just complained to me that he wants some security from your kind," Nolan said, sitting back down.

The Indian and Jethro looked at each other. They both realized that both of their groups were less of enemies to each other than they both were to the governor and sheriff.

The Indian nodded at Jethro. Jethro turned to Nolan, incensed

"Let me rephrase," Jethro said to Nolan. "My workers do need protection from the Indians. What we need is for the Marshalls and deputies to stop pushing them into attacking us as we work on the railroads!"

"Excuse me?" Nolan asked.

"You could take some time to try and map out the routes that we build so they're not going right through Indian territories. I would be unhappy if the Indians lit a sacrificial bonfire using my home! Stop pushing them into the warpath, governor!"

The Indian patted Jethro on the shoulder. Nolan got up and walked up to Jethro.

"I blame you and Hatcher for the Indian's actions."

"Huh," Nolan said, looking up as if he was thinking.

Nolan punched Jethro hard in the abdomen and knocked the wind out of him. Ralph and a deputy ran up to Jethro and roughly wrestled him out of the room.

"Now," Nolan said, turning to the Indian, "I didn't accept you here to draft a peace treaty. I hate the Indians. You're all savages. Your very being threatens the pure nature of this country."

Nolan brought himself very close to the Indian and whispered.

"I will not stop until there are no more Indians left," Nolan promised. "I will eradicate you."

Nolan took a big elbow to the jaw from the Indian and he got knocked over. The Indian pulled out a knife that was carved from a stone and he took multiple rounds in his body from the deputies. The Indian dropped the knife and fell down. Nolan got up and scrambled out of the way.

"See what I mean?" Nolan asked the deputies. "They're so sensitive."

Rod was actually really scared for the first time in his time with Derek and the gang. They were on their way to an Indian camp. Rod was actually less afraid of what Stanley would do if he found out that he was at an Indian camp than what the Indians could possibly do to him. If there was one thing Rod actually believed from the governor and sheriff, it was that the Indians were dangerous.

Rod never expected any cowboys to interact in a friendly way with any Indians. He was used to hearing and seeing the Indians fighting cowboys, the Indians fighting railroad workers and miners, Indians fighting deputies and Marshalls, and Indians fighting with freed slaves. Rod was led-on to believe that the Indians were after everybody, and it really seemed that way.

But, one thing that seemed natural about the experience so far was that Derek was a very good friend to the Native American. That made perfect sense to Rod, and it made perfect sense to Tom, Tex, etc. But, this part of Derek was one of the things that the guys were in the dark about. No one understood why Derek was so close to the Indians, especially a tribe that was as aggressive and ferocious against whites as the Apache. Derek never opened up about that, and the whole gang was persistent in trying to figure out his history with the Indians. But, Derek was such a rebel that it wasn't out of character for him to have such an unlikely ally as the Apache Indians.

The subject of the Indians was another touchy-subject between Derek and Tom. Outside of the gang, Tom trusted absolutely no one. Of course, he had his reserves about new members and young guys, but if they weren't riding with them, Tom expected treachery, lies and backstabbing from anyone else. Tom wasn't one who believed in combining forces. It had nothing to do with them being Indians; it had to do with them not exclusively being in their gang all the time.

The first glance at the camp was exactly was Rod expected. A big dirt patch underneath a huge canopy of leaves in the high trees. Here were many small shelters made of sticks, animal skins, mud and clay. There were a lot of men making weapons out of wood and stones, and the religious leaders doing rituals and ceremonies. Rod did like the trees; they were great for climbing.

Their welcome wasn't quite like the one they received at "Maim Street." The Apaches actually had work to do and responsibilities to take care of. A few Apache men were getting ready to go out on a hunt and just passed Derek by, giving him a quick wave.

Rod had never such fit and healthy people. He never gave himself the credit for being athletic and strong, but these guys lived like him every single day, on top of fighting for their lives constantly. They were all tall, had big chests, cut abs and large arms. They also had the mentality of warriors/survivors. Rod didn't see one smile on any of the men. They were all serious.

"Okay, we've made our appearance, Derek," Tom said, walking with stiff arms and looking straight ahead. "I think we can go now."

"Don't be ridiculous, Tom," Derek said, stopping in the middle of the camp. "That would be rude."

Rod took off his brand new cowboy hat that was made for him by Jess while they were in "Maim Street." It was like Derek's; it had the similar color and shape, only Jess curled the side up all the way to the hat. Rod liked the look with his long hair out of the sides. Jess gave it to him right before they left.

Once Rod had his hat off, he looked up at the canopy of the forest treetops. He thought he saw a person hanging upside down in the trees. Whatever it was dropped, did a back flip and landed right in front of Derek.

It was an Indian, and he was the type of Indian that Rod was waiting for. He was even bigger, thicker and more muscular than the rest of the men. He had scars all over the place from fights.

"How are you doing, Pacquio?" Derek asked.

The Indian just stared at Derek.

"Oh, I'm sorry," Derek said. "My mistake."

Derek started talking to Pacquio in Native American. Rod looked around at the expressions in the gang to see if that surprised anyone as much as it surprised him.

"It blew my mind when I first heard this," Tom said to Rod.

Derek turned back to the gang after he and Pacquio finished speaking to each other. The whole conversation, Pacquio seemed like he was about to lash out at Derek but he was as calm as can be.

"He's just got some ants in his pants on account of..."

Pacquio whacked Derek in the back of the head and turned to walk away. Tom ran up and palmed Pacquio in the temple and knocked him over. Pacquio got up enraged and he and Tom grappled with each other. It was harder for Tom because Pacquio wasn't wearing any clothes for him to grab onto.

The gang and a group of Indians tried to break it up. Derek was a good sport and didn't take any cheap-shots at Pacquio while the melee was going on.

The whole spectacle was abruptly interrupted when a loud thud of wood on wood broke out around the campsite. Everyone turned to what looked like the chief's tent. It was the chief's tent. It was built on a raise, it was put together much better than the other tents and the man standing in the threshold looked like a chief. He was an older man standing tall and strong with a big cape made of bear fur. He had big dream-catcher earrings and he was holding a big staff.

"Pacquio," the chief boomed in a very serious voice, "fetch us some water from the river."

"I'd do what he says," Tom said to Pacquio. Pacquio looked to Derek for a translation. Derek said something in Native American that got Pacquio thrashing to get after Tom.

"He got all worked up over that?" Tom asked Derek.

"I told him that you said your tree was twice the size of his tree," Derek said. "Think about it."

Tom fake-laughed that Derek told Pacquio Tom said his penis was bigger than Pacquios.

"Should we come back another time, chief?" Derek asked. "It seems like everyone is a little high-strung. By 'everyone' I mean just Pacquio."

"You and your tribe are always welcome in our land," the chief said, warmly but still seriously.

"You still haven't explained that we're not related to each other?" Tom said to Derek. "I will continue to be offended as long as he thinks we're brothers."

"And he'll be offended every time you shit yourself when he approaches you," Derek responded. "New guys, this is Chief Alo. If you ever need to know anything about anything, he's your guy. I swear to God, and all the mountain and sun gods, that he will have an answer for you. Go ahead, Marcus, ask him who the Wyoming rodeo champion is?"

Before Marcus even opened his mouth, Chief Alo had an answer.

"Derek," he said, grinning.

"See how good he is?" Derek asked the guys.

"Derek, while your men get settled in our great domain, we need to have a talk."

"Sure thing," Derek said, jogging toward his tent. "Guys, get your fill of the peace-pipe."

Derek joined Chief Alo in his tent and sat down.

"How have you been, wise-guy?" Derek asked, taking off his hat. "How's the hunt been? The sheriff's department has really been racking in the buffalo lately. It's those uniforms."

"Derek," Chief Alo said, sitting down, "I know you were never one for our philosophic ways, but I have been seeing signs form the gods."

"You can't let the gods tell you what to do, Chiefy," Derek said. "I don't even let other people control me. I'm gonna let beings that can't even show themselves to me tell me what to do?"

"When will it be enough for you, Derek?" Chief Alo said. "What will it take for you to be satisfied?"

"I feel like I've been satisfied since the Civil War, Chiefy," Derek argued. "I don't know what you're talking about."

"Stop running away from your problems, Derek," Alo said. "You're suffering over Jess…"

"Next question," Derek said. "I'll talk about anything else."

"You didn't just appear from the sky a lonely boy," Alo pestered. "You had a family and you obviously have demons with them you haven't put to rest."

"Pass," Derek said. "Something else."

"You need to start healing somewhere," Alo said.

"We'll get one down the line," Derek said. "Keep shootin 'em at me."

"Settling down?" Alo asked.

"In what sense?"

"Something of a steady home," Alo suggested.

"Steady, to me, is another word for dead," Derek said.

"Why do you refuse to let anyone help you?" Alo asked.

"I don't need no help, Chief," Derek said. "Why fix what ain't broken?"

"I am honored that think of us as your family and you come to us for assistance against the Wyoming government," Alo said, "but you can't keep dodging bullets and cheating death forever. You're going to get old like me and life will catch up with you."

"I've seen you wrestle with some of the men," Derek said. "You've got at least another fifteen, twenty years before your age starts to disagree with you."

"I'm flattered that you think so," Alo said. "What do you need right now?"

"I'm sure the Apache have been feeling the increased pressure from the sheriff's department?" Derek asked.

"It's worse than ever," Alo agreed.

"I think that your forest-stalking strategy could use a few good weeks of rough-and-tumble cowboy brawling," Derek said. "My guys are the best in the business, as you know."

"I love seeing Tex trap a guy in some kind of enclosure," Alo said, grinning. Derek laughed.

"Yeah, that's the best, Chiefy! I'm positive Roth will have some more deforestation and unnatural forest fires to flush your people out of their homes. We'll hit 'em with a double-edged sword this time."

"I'm looking forward to it," Alo said.

"Oh, one more thing," Derek aid after he got up.

"I'll keep Pacquio on the hunt and away from the camp as long as your gang is here," Alo promised.

"It's not that," Derek said. "Let that cry-baby as close to me as he wants to get. I personally brought a new, young guy along. He's a really great kid. Name's Rod McGillis. He got desperate in the face of his father not being able to pay for necessary medical procedures and to keep his farm from foreclosing. I want you to give him spiritual guidance so he doesn't end up like…. Me."

Derek darted out of the tent before Alo could try to explore Derek's feelings.

Everyone in the gang obviously knew about Derek's feud with Pacquio, the champion warrior in the Apache tribe. At least, he was as far as the gang knew. No matter how nice and easy-going Derek was to Pacquio, the Apache just could not stand Derek. Pacquio didn't have anything against any other member of the gang, not even Tom. It was just Derek that he despised, and for seemingly no reason on the surface. Everything Derek did, Pacquio tried to do it ten times better and faster. It was almost like Pacquio felt the need to compete with Derek and prove to the tribe that he was better than him.

The feelings of hate weren't mutual with the rest of the tribe. The entire tribe liked Derek almost as much as the people of "Maim Street" did. The Apache were very relieved to finally find a group of whites that they could trust, and did everything they could to stay in Derek's favor.

Rod noticed that Derek had an interesting dynamic between himself and Chief Alo. Rod assumed that Derek never made much of a son in his past; he was too rebellious to be parented correctly. But, Derek and Alo had something of a father-son relationship. They had the appropriate age gap between them. Derek always appeared to go to Alo when he had a problem, and Alo always obliged to guide him. The chief's name did translate to "spiritual guide." Rod felt like that's what he and Stanley had, except that Stanley would seek Rod out and just assume he needed some advice. Everything Stanley taught Rod he appreciated, whether or not he agreed with it. Rod felt like everything Stanley talked about was worth knowing. That's what it was like between Alo and Derek. Even if Derek would storm out and avoid an exchange with Alo, Derek knew Alo was always right, even if Derek didn't want to hear it. Part of Derek's lone-wolf style was that he liked to be right and hated being wrong. But, Alo could make him realize that he was wrong like nobody else. Alo was even good enough to get Pacquio to shake Derek's hand every now and then, but it was always a very brief truce.

Rod quickly learned to love the Indians against his father's assumptions. But, Rod could totally understand that it would be scary if any of the Apaches, even if was a woman or a kid, was attacking him. But, as long as they weren't, Rod had no problem with them.

Rod was finding that the Indians were like him in every way. They loved being outside, they loved enjoying raw nature, and they knew how to preserve nature. Rod fit right in when he took kids out to hunt or worked on totem poles with men and women. The whole culture of the Indians intrigued Rod and seemed like a lot of fun and made a whole lot of sense. They were people of the earth and nature, so why not pray to and worship elements of nature? Rod was loving it.

The Indians also knew how to have a good time in a much more healthy way than the whites back in town. Rod looked back on all his hollow, empty trips to the bar and felt like he was missing out on the fabulous group dances, songs and parties. Rod made a point to try and remember a few of the Apache dance moves so Molly could learn them. She would like that.

The Indians also knew what was important in life. There was only one planet earth and they knew how to preserve it and utilize her resources responsibly. Not like the whites that had to mine as far into the ground as they could and take everything out or wipe-out the forests and pollute the air with gasses just to make some money. The real money, Rod learned, was within family and friends. Rod thought the McGillis' were closely-knit, but the Indians were great family people.

Rod also saw the value of capitalism and rugged individualism being disproven and appropriately mocked in the Indian tribe. Outside the wife and kids, the Indians had no relations to each other. That didn't stop them from treating each other like family and sharing their happiness with each other. The Indians took care of each other and helped everyone keep up. For example, one Indian got violently ill before a big hunt. The other Indians each sacrificed a portion of their kill and donated it to the Indian's family. That was creating a more stable and successful society than Rod was seeing from the actions of the barons of industry in the white lands. The "civilized whites" seemed more like savages than the Indians. Rod kept forgetting that he was living among the "violent", "warring" Apaches. He didn't see that at all.

Rod had started a totem pole with a group of young Apache girls that wanted to make one on their own, without any boys or men helping.

They allowed Rod to help because he was a white outsider and wanted to show him their ways of life.

One of the girls was on the top of the totem pole, leveling out the top. Rod had another girl on his shoulders so she could paint the top face of the totem pole, an owl's face in honor of their chief.

All the young Indian girls reminded Rod of Molly. They all had her long black hair and they were all self-empowered like her. All the Indian women reminded him of Sally because of the same reasons.

"Young Rod," Chief Alo said, walking up to Rod.

"Yes, sir," Rod said, shaking his hand.

"I'm a regular person," Alo said. "Call me by my name."

"Okay, Alo," Rod said.

"Ever been inside an Indian's tent before?" Alo asked.

"Squanto or somebody has given me some space for the last week," Rod said.

"That's fine," Alo said. "Would you like to take a look around mine?"

"Yeah, absolutely," Rod said.

Rod took the first Indian girl off his shoulders and then brought the other girl off the top of the totem pole.

"Did you happen to look at the top animal's head we carved?" Rod asked Alo on the way to his tent.

"I sure did," Alo said. "I'm very grateful."

Alo and Rod entered his tent. Rod had never seen anything like it. The entire tent was engulfed in a light, warm mist that, every time it was breathed in, it cleared the throat and rejuvenated the senses. It wasn't like the disgusting tobacco that everyone smoked at the bars. Alo's stuff actually smelled good and made you feel good.

There were designs all over the coating around Alo's tent. There were paintings of buffalos, bison, eagles, falcons, mountain lions and rams. There was painting of an Indian that Rod assumed was Pacquio; a large man holding up the head of a cougar. Then, there was one of a group of Indians sitting around a big feast and they were all waving in what looked like a young boy with a cowboy hat. His face wasn't colored in because he was white. Rod could only imagine that was young Derek.

"Who is this guy, Alo?" Rod asked.

Alo looked over after concocting some kind of natural drink.

"That would be Derek when we first met him," Alo said, taking a sip of his drink. "Have a seat."

Rod sat down across a small fire from Alo.

"Have you grown comfortable with the American Indian thus far?" Alo asked, passing his drink to Rod.

"Grown comfortable?" Rod asked, taking the drink.

"You were nervous when you first came here," Alo reported. "It's okay, my people get nervous around whites. It's a shock. You're not a hater. Perhaps your environment taught you some falsehoods about Indians."

"Actually, my father fought Indians in the Civil War," Rod said.

"Union soldier, right?" Alo said.

"That's right," Rod said.

"A lot of the Indian tribes wanted to help the Confederacy because they liked a divided America," Alo explained. "I forbid my tribe from participating."

"I guess I was a little taken aback when I first got here," Rod said.

"I read people, Rod," Alo said. "You were scared. There's nothing to be embarrassed about."

"Well, I feel like one of you now," Rod said.

"That's great," Alo said. "I'm glad to hear it. So, joining Derek's gang?"

"Not long-term," Rod said.

"Why not?" Alo said.

"Because…. I've got my old life to get back to."

"Obligations?" Alo asked. "Duties?"

"I guess," Rod said. "But that's how I think of my family."

"Ah, you're close to your family?" Alo asked.

"Very close," Rod said. "Except for maybe my father. Sometimes I'm not sure."

"Stop," Alo interrupted. "Has your father ever hit you?"

"Never," Rod said defensively.

"Does he seem to constantly teach you about things that you don't know about?"

"Yes, always," Rod said.

"You and him are close," Alo said. "You and he? I have not mastered English yet."

"You're better than a lot of people back in town," Rod said.

"Now, I allowed you to stay in my land and showed you a lot of generous hospitality, have I not?"

"You've all been great," Rod said. "People in my own race don't even treat each other like humans."

"Well, I need you to do something for me in return. Very small thing, I think it's reasonable. I want you to never lose your connection to your family. Everything you do, don't forget about the reason you're doing it for your family. Don't get lost in greed or anger. Hold onto your family. Otherwise, you'll be wandering through life without a purpose, never able to find peace."

"Did Derek tell you to talk to me about this?" Rod asked.

"I won't tell anyone what you said to me in here," Alo said. "I need to maintain the same honor to everyone else I guide."

"I can appreciate that," Rod said.

"So, I need an answer," Alo said, "and I'll give you an Apache name."

"I will always be thinking about my family," Rod said.

"You know what that makes you?" Alo asked. "The Alpha-Bear."

"Why is that?" Rod asked.

"Because the Alpha-Bear takes care of his family," Alo said. "Just like you."

"Chief, you better get out here!" Derek shouted.

Alo got up and he and Rod left the tent. They found a bunch of people standing around the Apache that was sent to meet with the governor. He had been badly beaten.

"What happened, my son?" Alo asked, walking up to the Indian and observing his wounds.

"The sheriff had people follow me," the Indian said. "I think they know where we are."

All the men in the tribe looked ready to go to battle.

"I'm sorry, my chief," the Indian said.

"The last thing you should be is sorry," Alo said, sprinkling some powder on the guy's face. It was obviously something to keep the cuts from getting infected.

"Why don't we give them him?" Pacquio shouted, getting Derek in a headlock and putting a knife to his throat. That was the only English Pacquio knew, and he had been practicing ever since he met Derek to say that perfectly.

Derek wasted no time. He flipped Pacquio over his shoulder and took the knife from Pacquio.

"I came here to help you," Derek said. "You know you need us to defeat the sheriff. You can't do it on your own. Look how much progress you've made. No offense. I'm willing to g into battle with you."

Derek flipped the knife so the handle was facing Pacquio.

"How about you?" Derek asked.

Pacquio took the knife and Derek gave him a hand up.

"Everyone, prepare for battle," Chief Alo said.

All the Indians and cowboys immediately started scrambling to prepare to fight the sheriff.

"Are you gonna prepare for battle?" Derek asked Alo.

"They didn't used to call me 'general' Alo for nothing," Alo said.

"Ha, ha!" Derek yelled. "I'm excited."

The local sheriff had the state militia with him this time, not just deputies. They all paraded like British soldiers in the Revolutionary War through the thick forest, seeking for the Apache tribe that they had been stalking for a long time. Alo's tribe, like Derek's gang, was the tribe that gave the governor the most hell. Alo had a bounty on his head that was close to the bounty on Derek's head.

What the militia didn't know was that they had already been seeked-out by the Apaches. They were in the treetops, in foxholes, in puddles of mud, and hiding behind rocks. The militia members were constantly walking right by and looking at the Indians, and disguised cowboys and not realizing it. Derek loved getting himself and the gang Apached-out for battle. There'd be no other time for him to run around in his underwear with his body covered in dirt.

Derek and Rod were both standing on high tree branches, pressed up against the base of the tree.

"Hey," Derek whispered to Rod. Rod looked over and could see Derek's shiny smile amongst the mud on his face.

"Seriously," Derek said, "when was the last time you've been butt-naked in a tree with mud all over you?"

"Derek," Rod whispered, "no one's butt-naked."

"Really?" Derek asked. "Well, I guess I'm gonna get away with it."

"Thanks for asking the chief to talk to me," Rod said.

"No problem, Alpha-Bear" Derek said. "It does everybody good to have a pow-wow with Chiefy. He knows what he's talking about. Look at this."

Derek pointed to a militiaman who was walking over to a ditch to take a piss. An Indian silently dropped out of the tree behind him and slit his throat. The Indian then silently climbed up the tree and disappeared.

"They're here!" a militiaman shouted, pointing to the dead body.

All the militiamen got their guns ready and they started looking in every direction of the forest.

"Keep your eyes open!" the sheriff yelled.

He turned around when he heard a whirling noise and a sling wrapped around his throat and locked up. He choked to death in an instant.

"Shit, they got the sheriff!" one of them yelled.

"We might as well run!" one of them yelled.

A militiaman walked up to a small creek and looked in. He saw the reflection of an Indian in the water. The militiaman looked to his left, where the reflection was. Nobody was there. The Indian had been under the water. Before the militiaman realized, the Indian sat up out of the water and shot a poison-tipped dart at the militiaman's throat and killed him. The

Indian went back underwater and breathed out of the reed that he used to shoot the darts.

Before the next slick attack happened, Pacquio burst out from under the pile of leaves he was hiding under and blew the whole operation. Pacquio was never one to fight like that.

Pacquio started howling his war-cry and went nuts on the militiamen. He ripped the rifle out of the nearest one's hand and bashed his head-in with it.

"Idiot!" Alo yelled when Pacquio was pinned behind a tree. "Attack!"

All the Indians and cowboys left their hiding spots and swarmed the militiamen.

Tex rammed one of the men who was pinning Pacquio into the three Pacquio was hiding behind. Pacquio sprung out and stabbed the militiaman in the throat. Tex threw his elbow back into Pacquio's face and then delivered a punch to another militiaman. The elbow was one hundred percent deliberate.

The militiamen never had a chance. Hey hadn't been trained to fight the Indians the way they fought. They had walked into a huge trap. That's what the Apache did best. Pacquio's outburst didn't do much to ruin the plan; Derek trained his gang to do best on a whim. Tom disagreed with that, though.

Tex did his usual thing for the first time that Rod saw. Tex was like a huge bear; when momentum got behind his big body, nothing could stop him and everyone on the receiving end of his force was out of luck. When he punched, it didn't matter what people held in front of their face. It could have been a hunk of metal and Tex would have punched through it.

Tom, contrary to his uptight, nit-picky personality that as extremely prone to feminine hissy-fits, he was a true tough guy. Rod knew exactly what was going through Tom's head when he was in a fight. The lawmen that were always trying to arrest him and the gang didn't care about Tom's girls and wouldn't lose any sleep if Tom was in a cell and not providing for them. Nobody was going to stop Tom from providing for his family, no matter how many badges they flashed him. Rod felt the same way about himself and his family. If Rod and Tom died trying to get money for their family, they could rest in peace knowing they did all they could.

Tom would have made a good Indian. He had the long hair and he looked even more ferocious in his war-paint than did Pacquio. The one thing about Tom was that he definitely let his emotions get the better of him whether it is frustration, urgency or anger.

Rod wished that he could have witnessed more of the Apache-style of warfare, but the brawl was exciting enough.

As the Indians and the gang chased the remaining militiamen away when the battle turned into a mismatch, Chief Alo was squaring off with a militiaman with the exact same build as him. They were also the same age.

"Did you assault one of my children?" Alo calmly asked, removing his animal-skin cape.

"I assaulted his ass and liked it," the militiaman confessed with a sick smile on his face.

Alo jammed the butt of his staff in the ground and pulled out a big stone-knife. The militiaman pulled out a big machete of his own. The Apache warriors and Derek's cowboys made a human arena around the two combatants. Only one of them was walking out alive and if it was the militiaman, he wasn't leaving the forest alive.

Pacquio was the craziest bystander. He was jumping a full body-length up in the air, waving his fists and cheering for Alo in the Apache language. Derek picked up on a few suggestions Pacquio had for Alo to do with the militiaman's organs.

The militiaman lunged forward and swung down at Alo's shoulder. Alo stepped aside and tapped the militiaman on the head with the handle of his knife. Derek started-up a big laugh.

The militiaman thrust hard at Alo's throat. Alo grabbed the militiaman's wrist and bent his arm behind his back. Once Alo decided the militiaman felt enough pain, he shoved him away.

He militiaman turned around and charged at Alo, waving slashes at him. Alo dodged all of them.

The militiaman took a foolish breather. Alo jammed his rough-edged knife into the militiaman's thigh. The militiaman dropped his machete and tried to pull the knife out. Alo hurled his machete into the forest.

"You think you're going to pull out a knife with an edge like that?" Alo asked. "And you think **my** people are uneducated?"

"I bet you didn't learn about knives in the private school with your sweater and stockings," Derek yelled at the militiaman.

"You savages!" the militiaman yelled.

"I don't mind people taking about me," Alo said. "They're just words. But, I don't take kindly to my people being insulted."

"They're all gonna hang," the militiaman promised. "Like all varmints deserve."

Alo turned to Pacquio like he was going to say something to him. Instead, he whirled around on his heel and shoved the knife into the militiaman's throat. The gang and the Indians cheered when the militiaman's body fell on the ground. Alo slowly pulled his knife out and cleaned it off. He quietly prayed to the gods for forgiveness.

"That was terrific!" Derek yelled. "Group hug!"

"He's nude!" Rod yelled. Everyone backed away from Derek. Derek walked toward Tom with his arms wide.

"Get away from me, freak," Tom said, walking away from Derek.

Derek started to pick up his pace and Tom started to run.

"What the hell, you sicko!" Tom yelled.

Everyone laughed as Derek streaked after Tom.

"I would have never noticed," Surge said to Rod.

There was going to be a hanging in Wyoming's capitol that day. Specifically, an Apache Indian. Even more, an Apache youth. He was around Molly's age and had gotten lost exploring. He had never killed anyone before.

With the exception of the thunderstorm that was just about to hit the capitol, the crowd there was very energetic and happy to see an Apache hanged. Admission to the event was free; even Nolan wasn't thinking about revenue at something like this. He believed that everyone should be allowed to enjoy a "savage" be executed.

This was the first thing that Stanley was able to drag himself out of bed for. Because Molly was starting to understand the bad things that were happening, Stanley wanted her to see this. Sally thought it was an awful idea, but she didn't want to aggravate Stanley in his condition.

Glenn got them good seats, like he usually did for the McGillis'. Stanley was extra-happy because he got to spend some time with Glenn's father for the first time in a long time.

The majority of the crowd was poor, but they didn't boo Nolan or Ralph's presence. This mob of poor laborers was excited to see the Indian die. Jethro's union decided not to go because they agreed that the Indians weren't the problem. But, their belief had yet to catch on with non-unionized workers. A majority of the workers in Nolan's state weren't unionized because they were afraid of what Nolan would do to them. Nolan constantly justified those fears. Jethro and his workers were the only few that decided to take some action. Overall, no one in Wyoming liked the Indians.

"It's good that we can all come together for something as appealing as hanging an Indian," Nolan said, pacing up and down the platform.

The crowd cheered. Nolan gave a thumbs-up to Ralph.

"Bring the little scum out!" Ralph shouted to two deputies.

The two deputies dragged a sobbing Indian child onto the platform. When Stanley first heard the boy's cries, he had flashbacks of the Apache's war-cry in the dead of night when their camps were constantly getting ambushed. But, once Stanley's mind was right again, he looked at the little

Indian through a whole new perspective. Stanley saw a defenseless, hopeless little boy losing all hope because he was about to die. Stanley had felt feelings close to that during the Civil War, and he understood what it was like.

"This is not right," Stanley mouthed to himself.

Stanley started feeling shamed to be standing in the crowd that was truly acting savagely as they waited with anticipation for the boy to die.

"Sally, they can't do this," Stanley said to her.

"Relax, Stanley," Sally said. "The boy won't be able to hurt any whites anymore or whatever he's done."

"No," Stanley said. "He's just a boy. They can't do this just because he's different."

"Wow," Sally said. "You're finally getting in touch with your conscience. I'm so happy for you."

"Molly," Stanley said, "people are not evil because they're different from you. You can't define an entire race by the actions of a few. I want you to look any Indian you see by whom he is on his own and not judge him by a few warriors."

"Are you drunk, Stan?" Glenn's father asked, chuckling.

Sally glared at Glenn's father. She never liked him; he was pretty heartless toward the Indians during his time as sheriff.

"You brought this upon yourself," Ralph said as he tightened the noose on the boy.

"Damn demon," Nolan said, punching the boy in the face.

"Governor, they seem like they can't wait for this anymore," Ralph said, looking at the restless crowd. They looked like they were about to flood the platform and rip the boy apart.

"Maybe we should break the boy's neck before they do."

"No speech from me, just do it," Nolan said.

"Are you ready to see this vermin die?" Ralph shouted. He crowd's behavior answered his question.

"Pull it!" Nolan shouted at a deputy.

A deputy released the lever and the boy's weak neck snapped when the rope straightened. The crowd went nuts.

"I can't be around this," Stanley said. "Let's get the hell out of here."

"I'm glad you feel this way, Stanley," Sally said, holding Molly's hand as they made their way through the insane crowd.

Stanley's opinion of the American Indian had taken a complete 180 degree turn when he saw that boy get hung.

Bolton Butler

There was only one other outlaw in Wyoming that had any kind of name besides Derek. That was Bolton Butler. Before Derek's gang really started to pick up speed and got on all the headlines, Bolton Butler's gang was the most wanted.

Bolton Butler and Derek hated each other. It wasn't like Pacquio and Derek where Derek couldn't care less about what Pacquio thought of him; the feeling of hate was mutual between the two outlaws. That was because Derek used to be in Butler's gang. From the start they hated each other. But, when Derek and Tom left Butler's gang and became the top dogs, Butler lost his mind.

Butler was an old type of outlaw that was dying. Derek was the new, up-and-coming outlaw that was going to replace the Butler-style outlaw.

It was true that people like Butler, were a sheriff's favorite outlaw. They weren't any good, and they couldn't do much damage against the law. Ralph enjoyed having Butler or any of his gang members in the cell for a day or so just to harass them and then let 'em go. But, Nolan was beginning to see something of a benefit from possibly working with Butler against Derek.

Butler and his whole gang were locked in the station in the capitol. Glenn was assigned the duty to give them their meal rations and clean up after them. None of these guys were going to waste food just to give Glenn a hard time cleaning up; they were all fat and were going to salvage any food they could get.

Especially Butler was fat. He wasn't fat like Tex where he had a lot of muscle and power behind him. Butler had the kind of fat that made him slow and lazy. He was also old. He had a bald spot on top of his head and a long, gray beard that made him look like a wizard. The only magic he could produce was a foul odor that could take the life out of anyone worse than Tex's gas.

Butler and his gang didn't even have the energy to verbally abuse Glenn while they were in the cells. They mostly just sat around and burped. The members of the gang actually hated each other, and especially hated Butler. It was the old kind of gang where every single member was truly out for themselves and cutthroat. That didn't make for good coordination in the gang. Derek's gang had no problem with that; everybody was great friends and worked well together. Butler's system of turning the gang against itself was a mistake Derek wasn't going to repeat for his gang.

"Glennwillie," Ralph said, walking into the station with Nolan, "they're out."

"Yes, sir," Glenn said, taking out his keys and looking for the one to Butler's cell first.

Ralph ran up to Glenn and shoved him face-first into the bars with a choking grip on his neck.

"I say to do something," Ralph snarled, "you do it. Right then. I don't like to wait."

"Sorry, sheriff," Glenn said, breathing fast.

"Got to it, then," Ralph said, letting go of him.

Glenn shoved the first key he had in his hand into the lock. Luckily, it was the right one. Butler left the cell first, and then all of Butler's men got into a fist-fight to be the next one out. Ralph's deputies broke it up.

"Fellas," Nolan said to the deputies, "keep an eye on the guys. Mr. Butler, I have an offer for you on my table."

The deputies and Butler's gang mingled together outside the station. It wasn't odd; they were two groups of criminals.

Back in the station, Glenn was re-evaluating his life and the career he was potentially going to be a part of. He was starting to think it wasn't for him, working for the sheriff.

Butler, Ralph and Nolan entered Nolan's office in the governor's mansion. Nolan sat down on his side of the desk and Butler sat down on the opposite side. Ralph stood off to the side.

Butler appeared to be searching for something on the governor's desk.

"What are you looking for, Bolton?" Nolan asked, grinning.

"You said you had something for me on your desk?" Butler said, in his really western-tangy voice. Nolan cringed just hearing it.

"It was a figure of speech, Bolton," Nolan said.

"Okay," Butler said, acting like he understood what Nolan said.

"Do you know what a figure of speech is?" Nolan asked, leaning forward.

"Is it important that I know?" Butler asked. "What's that outside?"

Nolan and Ralph, just to humor Butler, actually looked out the window. While they were turned away, Butler tried to steal a gold pen on Nolan's desk. Being the klutz that he was, Butler accidently knocked a bunch of papers off of Nolan's desk. Nolan and Ralph turned around and Ralph took the pen from Butler.

"You're not slick," Nolan said to Butler. "I hate to break it to you. You may have had things going for you when old-man Wilson was sheriff and I wasn't governor, but things are changing. You're not Derek Rhodes."

Butler slammed his fist on the table.

"Can you not say that name in front of me?" Butler asked. "Why don't we call him 'pissant'?"

"I can't argue with that," Nolan said. "Ralph?"

"I call him that all the time," Ralph said.

"Let's look at both of our options," Nolan said to Butler. "My government is going into serious debt because we're spending all this money on measures to defeat Rhodes, but he screws-up all the measures and takes all the money. On your hand, Rhodes has made a mockery of you and your gang. If we both continue at this alone, we'll have a bankrupt state and a once great outlaw will soon be a laughing-stock. I don't want that to happen."

"What's bankrupt?" Butler asked.

"Don't worry about it," Nolan said. "That's my problem. Let's worry about your problem. Is there anything you want more than to show Wyoming that you can beat Derek Rhodes and be a great outlaw again?"

"I want to do that," Butler said.

"I want that for you, too," Nolan said. "Now, quid pro quo. We'll need to work out an agreement if we're gonna help each other out."

"Wait, wait," Butler said. "Squid pro, what?"

"From this point forward," Nolan said, "if I say something that you don't get, forget about it. It's not that significant."

Nolan got a piece of paper out and started writing down a contract for him and Butler.

"I have signed this," Nolan said, using the pen that Butler tried to steal, "and by doing so, I agree that if you bring me Derek, I will pardon you of all crimes that you have committed or will commit in the future against the citizens of Wyoming."

Nolan slid the contract to Butler along with the pen.

"If you sign it," Nolan said, "you will agree to have no clashes with the sheriff's department or the state Marshalls. You are free to commit crimes on the citizenry of Wyoming, not the government. Can you do that for me?"

"So, we can't attack deputies or rob from bank accounts that belong to the Wyoming government?" Butler asked.

"Hey, look at how smart he is!" Nolan said to Ralph. "Correct! You can clean-out all the other accounts, just not mine. I need my hold on the banks, Bolton."

Bolton signed the contract.

"Excellent," Nolan said, shaking Butler's hand. "Ralph will equip you and your gang with any equipment you may need and you have the full assistance of the sheriff's department. Ralph, would you be so kind as to beef Butler's numbers up with some spare deputies?"

"Certainly, governor," Ralph said.

"You may go, Bolton," Nolan said.

Butler made his way toward the door.

"Wait, hold it," Nolan said, grabbing the pen and walking up to Bolton. He handed him the pen.

"You can have this for your troubles," Nolan said. "I know you want it."

"It's a good pen," Butler said, looking at it in his hand.

"Yes it is," Nolan said. "Now, we have no time to lose. Take as many deputies as you can gather and go after Rhodes!"

Butler excitedly left the mansion with his freedom to commit any crimes he wanted and with the extra help he needed to beat Derek.

"The very instant Rhodes is subdued," Nolan said to Ralph, "have Butler killed."

"Sure thing," Ralph said.

On the way out of the Apache camp, one of the young Apache girls gave Rod a bracelet she made out of thanks for helping with the totem pole. Inscribed on it in Native American writing spelled out "Alpha-Bear." Rod made sure to hang onto it so he could give it to Molly as a gift.

They left the Indian territory in the forest that they had just saved from destructions and made their way the planes, where they could do some hi-jacking of carriages and carts transporting valuable cargo.

There was a lot of activity on the planes while they were around. A lot of it was heavily-guarded and was accompanied by armed escorts. The gang rode with the convoys and performed many successful horse-bound robberies. They were able to rake-in a lot of loot in doing so.

This time, Rod didn't hold back. He took as much booty as he could carry, and it was a lot. As he was collecting the booty, he thought about how he wanted to give Stanley the best medicine and best procedures money could buy. He wanted to give Molly the most expensive, nicest clothes that existed. He wanted to take Sally to go out to eat where she didn't have to worry about the bill, just about eating as much as she could. And he wanted to get Sunny a doghouse and more toys than he knew what to do with.

Rod asked Tom if he was feeling the same way. Tom's answer affirmed what Rod expected and was essentially the same thing Rod was feeling. He wanted to send his daughter to a good school so she could grow up smart and be rich. He wanted to have enough money to make his wife feel like she was a queen in a palace.

Rod also asked Tom what it was like to be away from his family for so long all the time. Tom said it felt terrible. It made him feel like he was deserting his family each time, even though he was doing it all for them. Tom wished he could spend all his time with his wife and daughter, but then they'd have nothing to live on. Tom's father was a poor craftsman who couldn't give Tom any kind of life.

One of the carts they attacked had a press crew with it. Derek was a big attention-hog and loved to be in the spotlight. So, he left the press crew alive and made them take a bunch of goofy pictures of him and he gave them a bunch of quotes about what he thought about the governor and sheriff outright; they couldn't put any of them in the papers for concerns of appropriateness.

Derek staged a picture where he had a long pistol in his pants, creating the image that he had a gigantic penis. He took another one where he had a double-barrel shotgun in between his legs and they made one of the last living guards kneel down in front of him with his mouth wide-open. Tex, Villegas, Surge, Marcus and Otis were in the background with their faces wide with laughter. The whole time, Tom had a gun to the photographer's head, forcing him to abide to Derek. They owned the planes, and Tom wasn't worried about any deputies crashing their party. Tom was able to relax on the planes.

Derek as actually on good terms with all the media outlets in Wyoming. Being a people person, he was able to get on their good side and show them the real Derek that Nolan didn't want Wyoming to see. None of Derek's charm had any benefit, though. Nolan was very vigilant in controlling the press and only let them report what he wanted them to report. The truth never got out. No one satisfied the needs of reporters the way Derek did, and they appreciated that. Only the photographers got annoyed with Derek; he made them waste a lot of film capturing his crazy poses and antics.

Rod's favorite part of being on the planes was seeing his first real duel in person. Derek had deliberately left an armed guard alive during a gunfight so they could stage their duel once that guard was the last one left.

Derek had the quickest hands anyone had ever seen. He never bothered to even twitch his fingers before he drew. He even waited until the guy reached for his gun before Derek reached for his. When the challenger had the handle of his gun gripped, Derek had already drawn and put a bullet between his eyes. Rod knew no one could describe a duel the way it was live. Rod felt the entire world hold its breath before the men drew. Rod was incredibly nervous, but Derek appeared to be calm and cool during the whole thing.

On their last day in the planes, Rod felt like he did a lot of free-riding, the kind of riding that Derek recommended he do.

"That wasn't what I was talking about," Derek said, tuning his guitar. "Didn't you find it a nuisance to have to aim and keep your balance while you were firing your gun?"

"Yeah," Rod said.

"Trust me," Derek said. "Find some territory like this, just you and your horse, maybe your sister, too. She should enjoy it."

"My sister was really excited when you gave her your bandana at the rodeo," Rod said.

"Well, she seemed like such a sweet little thing," Derek said. "Trust me, you'll know when you ride for no reason."

Deep down, Rod knew that he hadn't done it yet. He was really antsy to do it at some point, and Derek wanted him to do it. Rod thought it was a good idea to bring Molly along to enjoy. If Stanley got better in good time, Rod wanted him to join him.

The gang had found the nearest town and had themselves a "Maim Street" style blow-out to celebrate their huge success on the planes. They got the whole town involved, everyone got drunk and the town was a total mess the next morning. Even Tom wasn't well enough to get everyone in gear.

It was terrible timing, too. Bolton Butler, his gang and the deputies had just arrived in town to find Derek.

Rod was just waking up from being passed-out on a porch outside a hooker club. He stood up and stretched his arms out. He saw blurs of cowboys on horseback. The blurs cleared-up into actual people.

"Are you with Derek Rhodes?" an old, fat cowboy asked Rod.

"Yeah," Rod said. Rod immediately wished he didn't say that when his vision totally cleared and saw that he had five deputies about to grab him.

"Derek! Tom!" Rod shouted as he tried to run into the hooker club.

The deputies grabbed him, threw him down the steps and onto the ground. Rod tried to get up and run, but one of the cowboys hit him in the throat.

"Derek Rhodes it's your old boss, Bolton Butler!" the old cowboy said, getting off his horse and firing two shotgun rounds into the air. "We've got the kid. You're gonna want to come out if you don't want him to feel some hurt!"

Butler fired off another round and a deputy and cowboy tied Rod's hands behind his back.

"You're working with criminals?" Rod asked the deputy. "You're supposed to be a lawman."

The deputy punched Rod in the face.

"There he is!" Butler shouted, looking on top of the roof of the hooker bar. Derek was standing up there.

"Let the kid go, Bolton," Derek said, sternly. "This is between the two of us."

"You brought the sheriff in on your side?" Derek asked.

"I have the governor, too," Butler said. "So give it up."

"What makes you think you're gonna stop me?" Derek asked. "You couldn't even stop Tom."

Butler snapped, and a deputy whacked Rod in the lower back with the butt of his rifle. Rod twisted his body in pain.

"The kid wants you to give yourself up," Butler shouted.

"You have no idea how strong this kid is," Derek challenged.

"I don't think you do, either," Butler said. "But, let's find out together."

The deputy repeatedly whacked Rod in the back.

"I've seen enough!" Derek yelled. "Now!"

Derek's gang all sprung out and started firing at Butler's gang and the deputies.

"I want to shoot you in the ass, Butler!" Tom yelled, using all his bullets to shoot at Butler. "Right in the ass, fat boy!"

"I got too much of a buffer zone!" Butler yelled. "Let's get the hell out of here. Grab the kid!"

Rod tried to run but he got mauled by a deputy and a cowboy. They tied him to a horse and Butler's gang took off. He deputies stayed behind to fight Derek's gang. They didn't have a chance.

Derek wasn't a part of the gunfight. He stayed up on the roof, trying to keep himself from crying that Rod was going to get tortured out of his mind because of Derek. Rod had no idea what Butler was going to do to him, and he didn't deserve any of it. Derek did, and he felt like crap that someone was going to receive his punishment.

"You're a tough kid," Derek said to himself, more to try and calm himself down than to give Rod spiritual aid.

"You'll fight your way out of it."

Derek wiped tears away from his eyes. This was the reason that he preferred being a loner. He was attached to his gang members and it affected him.

Tom ran onto the rooftop to find Derek.

"We killed all the deputies," Tom said, angrily. "Didn't let them get away this time. We made them all suffer."

"That's great, Tom," Derek said, wiping his face with his hat and getting up.

"What's the problem?" Tom asked.

"They've got Rod, Tom," Derek said.

"Aw, shit!" Tom yelled. "That's very, very bad! Derek, we both know that he's been growing crazy to nab one of us to screw with you. He's going to do something horrible to Rod to try and mess you up."

"We've got to find them," Derek said. "Right now."

Butler and his gang had something of a "Maim Street" but without the fun of Derek's "Maim Street." Butler's "Maim Street" was all maiming, no partying. It was exactly what it was like inside his gang. They were so dysfunctional and were on the verge of killing each other.

No one in Butler's "Maim Street" got drunk for the fun of it. They didn't do anything for the fun of it. Everything they did was to just maintain a certain level of insane violence. If Nolan really thought the Apache were savages, he should take a trip to Butler's town.

That night, Butler had his men just torture Rod for no reason at all. They weren't trying to get any information out of him; they just wanted to make his life hell for being in Derek's gang. Butler also wanted to let out some of his frustration that Derek was a much better outlaw than he was and at one point Derek took orders from him.

The first dose of pain consisted of two of Butler's cowboys driving Rod toward a fire and bringing his face ever so close to the flames so he'd feel it but not catch fire.

Rod was putting up a fight, just as Derek hoped he would. Rod dug his heels in the ground like he never did before and thrashed and twisted his body so it was as hard as possible for them to torture him.

"For god-dang-diddley sake," Butler said, disapprovingly with strips of bacon stuck between his teeth. "He's a kid."

"Do you want to do this, boss?" one of the cowboys snapped.

"Do you want me to take over because you can't handle a kid?" Butler asked.

"Fuck out of the way," the cowboy said, pushing the other away so he could handle Rod alone.

He drove Rod into the flames and held his face in there. Rod kept trying to pull his head away, but the cowboy held him there.

"That'll do, I reckon," Butler said.

The cowboy threw Rod onto the ground and stepped on his chest to hold him down.

"Don't ever think I can't take you on, boy," the cowboy said.

The cowboy gave Rod a quick little press on the throat and walked away.

"You ever been a rodeo clown, boy?" Butler asked Rod.

"Is this the stuff you're gonna do to Derek, if you catch him?" Rod asked, catching his breath. His face was still smoking hot from being in the flames.

"**When** I catch him," Butler corrected, "he's gonna be begging me to kill him. If God don't accept him, he'll beg the devil to let him in hell rather than deal with me again."

"You knew Derek when he was younger?" Rod asked, trying to seek-out Derek's full story.

"I sure did," Butler said. "The little bitch and Tom begged me to let them in my gang and the whole time they complained that I was unfair and mean. Fuck 'em. And Tom had the nerve to criticize me for being disorganized. He had to have been out of his mind!"

"Do you know anything about Derek beforehand?" Rod asked.

"Nothing," Butler said. "Only thing peculiar was he had that scar on his face from the beginning. Never told anyone where he got it from."

There were other whites besides Derek's immediate gang members that were allowed inside Alo's territory. They were Jess and Billy. Jess took Billy to Alo's land all the time. Billy was good friends with the young Apache kids, and Jess was in very close with Alo.

When Derek and Jess was a serious couple, he took her there all the time. Even Pacquio liked her. He liked her even more when he heard the news that she was finished with Derek. That was Pacquio's process of thought: he supported anything and everything against Derek.

Chief Alo was the first person Jess turned to for help when Derek left her. In the direct aftermath, Jess was an emotional wreck. She wasn't as self-assured as she was in the present day, so she took Derek's actions very hard. She thought it was her fault, and other things, but Alo consoled her and completely reframed her personality into a strong, powerful one. Alo didn't want her to have to depend on any man or anyone. Jess was fully capable of taking care of herself after her time with Alo. No one was going to break her spirits down now.

"Good to see you again, Pacquio," Jess said, walking up to him and shaking his hand. Pacquio gave her a friendly smile in return.

"Howdy, Pacquio!" Billy piped up.

Pacquio stuck his fist out at Billy and Billy bumped it with his fist.

"Billy, why don't you go play with the kids," Jess said, nudging him away. She turned back to Pacquio when Billy was gone.

"Chief Alo there?" she asked, pointing at his tent.

Pacquio pointed to the tent.

"Yeah!" Jess said. Pacquio nodded.

"Jess, great to see you again!" Alo said, emerging from inside his tent.

"Could I talk to you in there, please?" Jess asked.

"My tent is always open," Alo said. "I don't tie it shut for the literal and figurative meanings. Come on in."

Alo held the coating open so Jess could enter. Pacquio waited until Alo was inside his tent to hide under the tent and listen to their conversation. He could somewhat understand English, he just couldn't speak it except to suggest they sacrifice Derek to the sheriff.

"What do you need to convey with me, my daughter?" Alo asked Jess. "Always keep in mind you can tell me anything, it will wash right over me. Not that I'm not listening, of course."

Jess laughed.

"And anything you tell me will not leave this tent."

"I always trust you, Alo," Jess said. "Derek came by recently."

"Does that trouble you?" Alo asked. "You don't need him at all, Jess. You are your own person, and don't let anyone hold you down because you're a woman."

"You know," Jess said, sighing, "there were reasons that I liked Derek, and those reasons are still there."

"Yes, you agreed to marry him," Alo said. "You still feel some things for him, but not dependence."

"You got it, Alo," Jess said. "But, I met this new kid he has, and it just makes me worry for everybody that rides with him. All young kids are naive and impressionable. Even Tom has the vulnerability to be double-crossed by Derek."

"You're going a little too far about Derek, daughter," Alo said.

Jess liked it when he called her "daughter." It made her feel like Alo really cared about her.

"I know Derek's not that bad," Jess said. "I just want everyone to be okay."

"They are okay," Alo said. "I know the young man you speak of. You know what I call him?"

"What?" Jess asked.

"Alpha-Bear," Alo said. "That's because I firmly believe that that kid is never going to lose his desire to protect his family, like the alpha bear in the wild will defend his cubs at all costs. That kid and his family are going to be alright. Everyone in the gang is going to be fine. I wouldn't worry about it. But, the fact that you do worry affirms that you have a huge heart, and that's terrific. And Derek has a huge heart. It's his mind that needs some work."

Jess laughed.

"I guess that's how to put it with him," Jess said.

"Now, share a round of the peace-pipe with my people and then we will feast on the newest batch of buffalo," Alo said, standing up. "After Derek helped us fend-off the latest onslaught of industry and assault on mother-earth, the balance of nature has been better than ever."

"He can do great things," Jess said, leaving the tent with Alo.

"I assure you," Alo said. "If you were in any true danger, Derek would be there to rescue you."

That was the last thing Pacquio heard them say, and it was all he needed to hear.

"Remember when Tom tried to get us to-map out all of our missions?" a cowboy asked Butler.

"Oh, hell," another one agreed. "And then he thought he could actually get us to memorize them. He's crazier than a road-lizard."

"I couldn't believe Derek tried to be my friend," Butler said.

"Yeah, I'd never be your friend," a cowboy said, grinning. "You're a fat, disgusting prick."

Butler pulled out a gun and shot him in the face.

"Anybody else share that sentiment?" Butler asked.

All the cowboys stood up and pointed their guns at him.

"Yes," they all said in unison.

"I've been waiting to kill you, now I have the chance," one of them said.

"Not so fast," another cowboy said, pointing his gun at the cowboy. "I want to kill him."

All the cowboys started to argue with each other about who would kill Butler. Butler was too scared to move.

The arguing broke-out into fighting, and then gun-fighting. It happened; Butler's gang turned on itself. Derek and Tom predicted it.

To make things worse, Flaming arrows started to bombard the city. It was Derek's gang.

"Holy hell, run!" someone yelled.

Derek and the gang rode in when they got the town on fire. Butler's gang hated Derek more than they hated each other, so they decided to fight them. Butler took the opportunity to grab Rod and run for it. He didn't go very fast.

Butler made it to the forest with Rod and had to stop to catch his breath.

"I can see why you 'feel behind' in the game, Butler," Rod joked.

"Shut… up," Butler wheezed.

"Rod, where are you?" Derek shouted from the brush.

Rod could see Derek because the forest was lit-up by the burning town.

"I'm here, Derek!" Rod yelled, jumping into the air as high as he could.

Before Rod could warn Derek that Butler was right there, Butler grabbed Rod and put a revolver to his temple.

"Stop right there, Derek," Butler ordered as Derek joined them in the forest.

"Damn," Derek said.

To test Butler, he flinched the tip of the barrel of his revolver.

"Ah, ah, ah," Butler said, pressing the barrel of his revolver hard into Rod's temple.

"Sorry, kid," Derek said, tossing the gun aside.

"Don't worry about it," Rod said. "I've got this."

"I'd like to see you get this," Butler said.

"Here I go," Rod said.

Rod threw his head back and broke Butler's nose. Butler backed up and held his nose. Rod faced him and head-butted him in the face. Butler fell over and Derek kicked his gun away.

Derek had picked up his gun and ran over to Butler. Derek aimed the gun right between his eyes.

"Remember all the times you had the guys hold me back while you beat my ass?" Derek asked. "Well, the shoe is on the other ass."

"Wait, wait!" Butler pleaded.

Derek didn't want to listen to Butler grovel. He pulled the trigger and killed him.

"Fat shit," Derek said, pulling out a knife. He cut the ropes on Rod's wrists and released him.

"You okay?" Derek asked. "They didn't hurt you too bad, did they?"

"I'm fine," Rod said.

"Good," Derek said.

Derek gave Rod a tight bear-hug. Derek was relieved they didn't kill him or do anything irreversible.

The Train

Beverly Roth wished she didn't have to leave her real parents and go back to live with her uncle in the state capitol. But, she had no choice. Her parents felt the same way, but they didn't have a choice, either.

There was no possible way Nolan's brother and sister-in-law could take care of Beverly for a sustained period of time other than her frequent visits. They had lost everything, and didn't want Beverly to have to suffer with them. Beverly's father had Nolan's full support when his business was booming. Nolan gave him every kind of tax cut there was when he had money. When he lost it all, Nolan turned against him.

Beverly was on her way back to the capitol on the new Vanderbilt railway. She was accompanied by a personal bodyguard. Nolan instructed the guy to "not work too hard." Nolan had actually tried to lose Beverly a couple of times.

Nolan had a chance headed his way. The train Beverly was riding on was about the get hijacked and robbed by Derek's gang. They had no idea that the governor's niece was aboard the train.

Rod and Tex had positioned some TNT charges at a specific point on the railway and Tex was all set to detonate.

"Here they come!" Tom shouted at the bend of the railroad.

Tex propped himself up to push the lever. He thought a minute to himself.

"Rod, give it a shot," Tex said.

"Are you sure?" Rod asked.

"Positive," Tex said. "It's great fun."

"Alright," Rod said, rubbing his hands.

Tex moved out of the way and Rod got on the lever.

"Blow it up!" Tom yelled. "Pull it!"

Rod pushed the lever and the TNT blew up. The track was destroyed.

The train conductor started ringing an alarm bell to get the train's security moving and tried to hit the brakes in time. He didn't. The train derailed and Derek's gang pounced on the train.

The security forces all got shot as soon as they looked outside to see what happened. Rod was still really excited at detonating the TNT.

Inside the train, the bodyguard for Beverly had just woken up from a nap.

"Stay here," he told her, getting up and taking out a gun.

The bodyguard walked up to the nearest door of their train car and took a big right-hook to the face. He was knocked out.

"This is a pretty good one," Villegas said, taking the bodyguard's gun.

"Everyone relax," Derek told the train car. "We don't want to hurt anybody. We just want to rob you."

"If you can afford a ride on a train you can certainly spare a little something for a guy trying to feed his family, can't you?" Tom asked, shoving his gun in the faces of some rich old people.

Derek and Rod both took care of the other side of the train car as Tom and Villegas got the other column of seats.

Rod took the back-half of the seats. Derek noticed that Rod and Beverly were constantly looking at each other.

"Rod," Derek said, whistling at him, "conference."

Rod walked over to Derek.

"Do you know who that girl is?" Derek whispered to him.

"It's Beverly Roth," Rod said.

"The governor's niece, yeah," Derek said. "Now, it would be a little objectionable if it was me, but could you imagine how sexy it would be if an outlaw in my gang had a secret fling with her? Roth might have a stroke!"

"It's pretty good," Rod said. "But I don't think someone privileged like her would go for me."

"She doesn't look like someone who is happy with being privileged. Take my word for it. Girls like the bad-boy, Rod. Give it a shot."

"Alright," Rod said.

Rod went to the last seats in their column and took some jewelry from the women. Rod was starting to think he should ration what he took; he had more money than he could explain to his family that he got from a miner's pay.

Rod purposefully skipped Beverly's seat.

"Wait," she called out, taking her rings off. "Take these."

"I won't rob from you," Rod said to her.

"Why not?" she asked.

"Because you've got a pretty face," Rod said, taking money from some men in front of her.

Beverly blushed and Rod looked over at Derek. Derek gave him a thumb-up. Rod said something that he thought Derek would say. It worked.

"You're Glenn's friend, aren't you?" she asked.

"Glennwillie, as the sheriff calls him?" Rod asked.

"He hates that," Beverly said, laughing. "Well, if I can't give you anything valuable, can I invite you to sit down?"

She patted the seat next to her.

"Sure," Rod said, sitting down.

"Miss. Roth, I don't believe we've met," Derek said, walking up to them, "but I'm sure you know who I am."

"You're the Rhodes outlaw!" she said, excitedly. "This is so exciting."

"You do realize that your uncle probably wants to skin me alive and then shred me up, right?" Derek asked.

"I don't care what he wants," Beverly said. "I hate him."

"How do you like that?" Derek asked. "There is someone with brains in the Roth family. What do you think of that, Rod? You live closest to the governor out of all of us."

"I would have never guessed," Rod said.

"You're not Rod McGillis, are you?" Beverly asked.

"Yeah, I am," he said.

"I've seen your tax records," she said. "They're so unfair."

"You don't have to tell this guy twice," Derek said, slapping Rod on the shoulder. "This guy wasted no time in taking some action when his farm was in trouble. No sir, he got the money he needs back from your uncle and more."

"Well, take all of it," Beverly said. "It's yours, anyway."

"Well, I'm gonna get back to work," Derek said to Rod. "Take five."

Derek went back to robbing from the train passengers. Rod stayed with Beverly.

"You guys are definitely not like my uncle says you are," Beverly said.

"I think you spoke too soon," Rod said, watching Tex shoved his bare ass in the sleeping face of the Beverly's bodyguard.

"Derek, check this out!" Villegas said, laughing.

Tex ripped a fart in the bodyguard's face and woke him up. The bodyguard tried to scramble out of the stench-radius, but Villegas held him down.

"Give him another, Tex!" Villegas yelled.

Beverly laughed.

"He once cleared our entire camp doing that," Rod told her.

"Jesus, Tex," Derek said, waving the air in front of his nose. "You're not allowed to have fried chicken ever again!"

"I've got some ammo for you, Tex," Villegas said. "Chiles rojos."

"I really like your hat," Beverly said.

"Thanks," Rod said, putting it on her head. "I'm sure your uncle could have one specially made with the finest stuff if you asked him for one."

"He would never let me back in his house if he saw me wearing a cowboy hat," she said, putting it back on his head.

"Too bad," Rod said. "It looked good on you."

"Derek, our car is cleaned," Tom said, walking into their car.

"That's fine," Derek said. "Round up the rest of the gang. Chiefy Alo told me of a fabulous oasis-type-thing near these parts. We've got to hit it up."

"Let's go!" Tom shouted, walking through the rest of the cars and banging on the train walls with his gun to get everyone's attention.

"I've always wanted to see one of these places," Beverly said.

"Come with us, then," Rod said.

"Really?" Beverly asked. "You'd let me tag along?"

"Sure," Rod said.

"You got everything?" Derek asked Rod.

"Yeah," Rod said. "What do you say to Beverly coming with us?"

"Uncle Nolan's not going to be following a trail of bread crumbs after us?" Derek asked Beverly. "Sometimes the best bait is the best-looking bait, Rod."

"I would never go back home if I could," Beverly said.

"Come along, then," Derek suggested. "I'm sure we can show you a good time."

Just before all the outlaws left the train, Derek stopped to make a farewell to their victims.

"We appreciate all your donations," Derek said. "Good luck with... With everything."

All the outlaws got on their horses; Beverly rode on the back of Rod's horse.

"Fellas," Derek said, before they rode off, "we have a guest with us. Hiding behind Rod is Beverly Roth, the governor's niece."

"Great!" Tom said. "How much do you think we can get for her? One thousand? Two thousand? A Million?"

"Shut up, Tom," Derek said.

"He wouldn't give you anything for me, and he'd still think he got the better deal," Beverly said.

"She has the same opinion of the governor as we all do," Derek said, "so she's welcome with us. Nobody scare her or anything. After all, we're fun guys. Did someone ask about Alo's sweet-spot?"

"Finally!" Otis said.

"Right this way, gentlemen," Derek said, turning his horse toward the forest and riding off. Everyone followed him.

"Isn't Alo an Apache leader?" Beverly asked, nervously. Even as compassionate as Beverly was, she couldn't help being afraid of the Indians.

"He's a good friend of ours," Rod said. "Your uncle is lying about the Apaches, too."

Derek brought them all to a place in the forest with a lot of passive animals that weren't dangerous, a big cliff with a bunch of connecting, small waterfalls and natural pools, and hundreds of good trees for climbing. It was like a dream-playground for Rod. It was also a dream for Beverly because she had always wanted to be outside in a place like that but Nolan would never approve.

"I've never been anywhere like here before," Beverly said to Rod.

"I go to places like this all the time," Rod said, "and it never gets old."

Nolan demanded a meeting with the Vanderbilt spokesman after hearing the news that the train had derailed after it came across "bad" railing. Nolan knew that Beverly had gone missing, and truly did not care. He would have been happy if he wasn't so mad that the railroad was faulty.

"Here's the little flake, governor," Ralph said, shoving the Vanderbilt spokesman into the governor's office.

"I heard that old Cornelius has left us," Nolan said.

"Yes, he has recently deceased," the spokesman said.

Nolan snapped his fingers, and Ralph gabbed the spokesman by the shirt collar and shoved him down onto Nolan's desk.

"You cannot treat people like this!" the spokesman shouted.

"As it happens in my state," Nolan said. "You can. Well, we can. Not you. But, I digress. Would you like to join your former executive?"

"No," the spokesman said, shaking his head.

Nolan snapped, and let go of the spokesman.

"Then, for your benefit," Nolan said, "and for mine, carefully explain why you told me the railroad wasn't completed but your company told me that it was operational."

"It was completed," the spokesman said. "And it was operational. Vanderbilt's succeeding son took an investigatory trip down to the sight of the calamity. He found traces of explosive chemicals that are commonly used in TNT products."

"An outlaw attack," Nolan said to Ralph. Ralph nodded.

"My mistake," Nolan said to the spokesman. "I guess I didn't get the full story."

"You didn't the," the spokesman said.

"You may go."

"You want us to try and track down Beverly?" Ralph asked.

"You might do something important with your time," Nolan snapped. "Like successfully capturing Derek. Damn, things are not good if he's got explosives now. We don't really have explosives. This is bad!"

"Do you want to go to 'Maim Street' and see what they know?" Ralph asked.

"We'll pay a visit to 'Maim Street'," Nolan said, rubbing his forehead to relieve his stress. "Perhaps we'll even press Smart-Owl or whatever the hell he calls himself for information. If only there was someone really close to Derek that we could use to trap him. I guess it's effective to be an ass-wipe and not have anyone connected to you than to be charming like I am."

"Absolutely, governor," Ralph said. "You have many friends that would walk into a trap if you were in trouble. Not like Derek that everyone would leave for dead."

The place Alo recommended to Derek proved to be better than everyone expected. Alo knew everything about the woods, so they had high enough expectations for the place anyway. They were all surpassed by the reality.

Beverly was the most satisfied with the place because she had no idea what an outdoor paradise was like, so she had low expectations.

At one point, Tex almost emptied all the pools in the waterfall by doing a cannonball from the top of the cliff. Otis grossed a lot of guys out when he went shirtless and revealed all his permanent scars from being a slave.

Beverly definitely had the best time. She had never swam in a natural body of water before or climbed a tree, or been around animals at all. Nolan hated anything associated with the wild, even domesticated pets. He did accept vicious, trained hound dogs for use by the sheriff's department. But Beverly never got to pet an animal before. That changed when there were all the friendly birds and critters that weren't afraid of the humans at all.

Beverly also had a great person to teach her how to enjoy the outdoors. Rod took her up her first tree and took her to experience her first sunset without a window in the way. Beverly had also heard the best music in her life listening to Derek entertain.

Rod was a lot different from the rich kids that Beverly was forced to mingle with. Most of them were the sons of bankers or business tycoons that Nolan wanted to do work in Wyoming. Tall those kids were arrogant and rude to Beverly because of what happened to her father. Rod was totally different, and Beverly felt like the only woman in the state that was doing the things that she and Rod were doing. Nolan was doing his best to indoctrinate her into being a slave of a housewife. She hated it.

Derek was hoping that Rod was going to use Beverly's attraction to him to screw the governor over. But, Derek and Rod were different like that. Derek wanted Rod to have sex with Beverly and get her pregnant just so the governor would have to deal with having an outlaw-child in his family. Of course, only Derek was like that.

After their time in the forest, the gang decided that they had gotten more than they needed in their crime-spree and that it would be okay to take some extra time off. Derek wanted to meet Rod's family, but Rod wanted to be careful in case Stanley was ready to blow the lid off on Derek.

To make it easier, Tom and Tex said they would bring their families to the capitol so Derek would be less obvious. Apparently Tom's daughter was the same age as Molly, so that would have worked out. Tex, Tom and Derek all knew to stick to the story that they were all miners and to not call Derek by his name. They were just going to call him "Rick." They weren't nervous at all about going to the capitol and making a scene; they felt invincible after everything. Derek especially because he had killed one of his demons: Bolton Butler.

Hey also wanted to make sure that Beverly was taken care of and they dropped her off at the nearest working train station and then made a break for it before the train's security spotted them. Right before Rod left, Beverly kissed him.

Molly and Sally almost cried when they saw Rod return. Sunny almost lost his voice shrieking in excitement that Rod was back, and he was the first to get to Rod. Sunny lunged at Rod and knocked him down. Rod only gave Sunny a few seconds before he pushed him aside and got up to hug his mother and sister.

"Rod, we missed you so much," Sally said, almost choking Rod.

"Well, I don't think I'll be going anywhere ever again," Rod said. "The owner of the mine was a really generous guy and some outlaws we chased away left their booty behind, so we got ourselves a bonus."

"Take that stuff up with your father," Sally said. "I only care that you're back."

"Nice hat, Rod," Molly said, tugging on his shirt to get his attention.

"Yeah?" Rod asked, putting it on her head. "Have it, then."

Molly's head was a little too small for the hat and she took it off.

"I think this is for you, mama," Molly said, handing the hat to Sally. Sally put it on.

"Rod's back?" Stanley shouted from the front porch.

From first glance, Rod thought Stanley was in awful shape. His hair was messy from being in bed all the time, he was obviously weak because he was leaned-up against anything around him just to stay up, and his skin looked ghost-pale.

Rod ran up to Stanley and was about to hug him, but remembered that Stanley wasn't like that.

"It's good to be back," Rod said, sticking a hand out for Stanley to shake. Stanley looked at it and then looked up at Rod. He walked up to Rod and hugged him.

"Look at that, mama," Molly said, in awe.

"I know," Sally said. "I love it."

"I think the farm is going to be taken care of for a long, long time and the government will have nothing to complain about…"

"Hush-up about that, boy," Stanley said. "Have I ever told you that you're the best son a man could ask for?"

"You always seemed to project that idea but I've never heard it outright," Rod said.

"You're gonna hear it a lot now," Stanley said. "Because you are. By the way, not everything I told you may be correct."

"No?" Rod asked.

"No," Stanley said. "Indians are good people just like you and me. Well, that's fine because the owner of the mine was close to some Indians that taught us how to defend ourselves against outlaws. One of them gave me a bracelet which I think Molly would like. Also, ma got her hat because I was so good against an outlaw that I decided to take it from him."

"That a boy," Stanley said. "Molly, honey, your brother has a gift for you."

"Yeah, look at this," Rod said, walking up to her and showing her the bracelet.

"It's beautiful, Rod!" Molly said. "What's this say?"

"Alpha-Bear," Rod said. "That's what the Indians decided to call me because I... Because I worked in the mine to take care of my family like an Alpha-Bear takes care of his family."

"Yes, you do," Sally said.

Sally and Molly went to work preparing Rod a huge dinner because they assumed that the only thing he had to eat at the mine was gruel and hard biscuits. While they were doing that, Rod showed Stanley all the money he brought back with him. Stanley bought into the whole story that Rod got paid extra because he worked a lot of overtime and that he got a big share of the loot that the "outlaws left behind after the miners fended them off." The only truth that Rod told was that he spent time with the Indians. Stanley told Rod about his change of heart toward the Indians. Rod couldn't believe it.

Stanley was acting much different when Rod came back. Obviously, he was grateful that Rod did so much to save the farm and for him.

During their first meal with Rod in that long time, they asked Rod about the guys he worked with at the "mine." Rod decided to use the real characters; they were entertaining enough.

It turned out that Rod had enough money for the doctor to operate on Stanley, and the operation was successful. All of Stanley's directly medical problems were taken care of, and he fixed his own psychological problems by giving up on his hatred of the Indians.

So, everyone was happy. Even Beverly, for the first time in her life. While they were waiting for the guys to arrive, Beverly constantly snuck-out of the mansion at night to meet with Rod. Beverly also met Molly. Rod kept that meeting secret in the woods because he thought it might make Stanley go crazy if he found out that his son was dating the niece of the governor, a governor who could barely stand to have citizens in his state that weren't filthy-rich. The governor would definitely have Rod killed and spin it that a poor ruffian had kidnapped his niece.

Beverly and Molly hit it off right away. Like Rod was different from all the other boys Beverly was forced to be around, Molly wasn't like the arrogant rich daughters she had to spend time with.

"She's so pretty, Rod," Beverly said, watching Molly sleep with her head on Rod's shoulder as they looked at the clear night sky with all the stars shining brightly.

"Her mother must be beautiful."

"She sure is," Rod said. "My pa is a lucky one."

"Your whole family must be gorgeous," Beverly said.

"Well, my dad really just a big softy deep down," Rod said, "but he's not pretty."

"Deep down?" Beverly asked. "If you and Molly are his kids he must be a sweetheart."

"That's our mother," Rod said. "My pa wants everyone to think he's a tough guy. He's been one big firework of emotions lately."

"Because he missed you?" Beverly asked.

"Because I saved his life," Rod said.

Beverly was about to start crying, but Derek showed up in the forest.

"We're all here," Derek said. "How are you doing, Bev?"

"Better than ever," Beverly said. "I've been away from that monster of an uncle and out in the real world with real people."

"I'm glad to hear it, honey," Derek said. "Rod, I like that bandana your sister has around her neck."

"He gave it to her when he broke the rodeo record," Rod explained to Beverly.

"Congratulations, Derek," Beverly said.

"Unfortunately I didn't have time to collect my prize," Derek said. "The sheriff, you know."

"Yeah, I do," Beverly said.

"Let me go put this away and then I'll catch up with you at the bar," Rod said, standing up with Molly in his arms. She started to wake up.

"Molly, I'm bringing you back home now," Rod told her.

"Okay," Molly said. "Bye, Bev. Nice to meet you."

"Yeah, Molly," Beverly said. "Let's spend some more time together."

"Derek, don't be around my pop too much until I get him really drunk," Rod said.

"I can do that."

"Don't wait up," Rod said.

Rod brought Molly back toward the farm. On the way, they were met by two Apache men that Rod recognized from Alo's tribe. Molly's natural reaction was to be scared and she gripped Rod tightly.

"Guys, it's been a while," Rod said.

"Rod, isn't that your bracelet?" one of them asked.

"You're the Alpha-Bear," the other said.

"I wouldn't be the Alpha-Bear if it weren't for this angel right here," Rod said, lifting Molly up a little higher.

"Molly, these are the Indians that taught us…. They helped us fight the bad people."

"Thanks for looking out for my brother, guys," Molly said.

"Alpha-Bear always welcome with us," one of them said. "We must go, Alpha-Bear."

"So do we," Rod said. "I'll catch you later."

"They were so nice," Molly said to Rod.

"I know," Rod said. "Pa was wrong about them. What about Beverly?"

"She's quite a catch, Rod," Molly said. "You hang onto her."

"I'm not letting someone as great as her go," Rod said.

Rod brought Molly into their room and put in her bed. He went downstairs to find Stanley getting prepared to get drunk at the bar.

"My mining buddies are here, pop," Rod said.

"Alright," Stanley said, getting up. "I can't wait to meet 'em."

Rod and Stanley walked out of the farm.

"I'm serious, Rod," Stanley said. "What you did for me, the farm, and the family was phenomenal. I don't know of any sons that would do that for their father, even one who was as rotten as I was."

"You weren't rotten, pop," Rod said. "Not rotten at all."

"When you came back was the first time I hugged you," Stanley said. "I was horrible. I promise I'm gonna be different from now on."

"Same, different," Rod said, "it's all good."

Rod and Stanley found the entire town except the bar to be living. They walked in and all of Rod's "mining" buddies raised their glasses to them.

"You've got to be Rod's pop," Tom said, walking up to him.

"Yeah, Stanley," Stanley said, shaking his hand.

"Tom," Tom said, shaking his hand.

Tom wasn't close at all to being a known outlaw, so he could throw his name out in public.

"Rod, my wife and daughter are over there if you want to meet them," Tom said.

"I sure do," Rod said. He handed Tom some money.

"Order my dad whatever he wants."

"Hey, what a fabulous son I got!" Stanley said, going over to the counter with Tom to meet Tex, Villegas and Surge. Surge immediately started asking him questions about his leg.

Rod introduced himself to Tom's wife and daughter. Sure enough, they were just like Sally and Molly, so they got along very well with Rod. Rod promised Tom's daughter that he'd have her meet Molly.

After Rod said his "hellos" to all the guys, he sat down as far away from the Stanley as he could so Beverly could run up and sit on his lap, which she did.

"I told you she'd go for you, Rod," Glenn said, sitting down at the table with them.

"He put in a good word for you," Beverly said to Rod.

"That's my man," Rod said. "Shouldn't you be at work right now?"

"I deserve one night off, don't I?" Glenn asked.

"I've been telling you this for… I don't know, five years," Rod said.

"Well, I'm putting my foot down," Glenn said. "If Ralph don't like it, he can choke on his own awful breath."

"I like this Glenn," Rod said.

"I'm glad you're standing up for yourself, Glenn," Beverly said, "but don't oversell it. I don't want Ralph to hurt you. He will."

"He's done plenty of shit to me already," Glenn said. "I think I've been numbed-out."

Once Stanley was totally drunk out of his mind, Rod decided that it was okay for "Rick" to emerge. Derek couldn't help but talk about how close he and Rod got "in the mine." Stanley liked Rod the best.

Just as Glenn feared, Ralph noticed his absence for his shift at the station. He dispatched two deputies to check the bar. Unfortunately for them, there was a small group of drunks that the bar-tender hired to finally keep the sheriff out of his bar. The bar-tender had enough of the sheriff scaring his customers away and shaving his profits.

"No entry for you," one of them said as the whole group blocked the door for the two deputies.

"Get the hell out of here or we'll have this freak-show shut down," one of the deputies threatened.

"Get out of here or we'll beat the hell out of you," one of the guards said.

"Make us," one of the deputies said.

"With pleasure."

The group jumped the deputies and took them around back to give them a more thorough beating.

Stanley liked "Rick" so much that he actually asked him to come by the farm to have a dinner with the family. Rod thought it would be okay, do Derek agreed.

Unfortunately, while Rod was in the forest with Molly, Beverly and Tom's daughter, the governor and sheriff were mass-distributing wanted posters of Derek in as big a zone as they could because they only assumed that Derek and his gang did that stuff to the deputies. A poster made its way into Stanley's hands while Rod was gone. Stanley figured out who "Rick" really was, and the truth behind Rod's days "mining."

Derek showed up at the farm as the sun started setting. He was a little surprised when Stanley didn't act as friendly as he did at the bar.

"Yeah, I'm a little hung-over, too," Derek said, sitting down at the dinner table.

"Rod, I didn't figure your sister would be so striking by looking at you," Derek joked. Molly and Sally laughed.

"Well, she is," Rod said.

"Were you the senior-miner or something, Rick?" Sally asked, bringing the food in.

"I sure was," Derek said. "I like to take the new guys and take them under my wing because, you know, the mines can be dangerous for first-timers. Rod is definitely my favorite protégé in some time. He's a quick-learner and a hard-worker."

"That's our Rodney," Sally said. "Well, dig in, everybody."

Stanley took the big spoon in the mashed potatoes and piled it real high on his plate, glaring at Derek the whole time.

"Now, Stan," Derek said, "I know what's on your mind. The last time I had that beer I recommended to you, it had a whole different flavor. I don't know what that goofy bar-tender was thinking."

Stanley still just glared at him.

"I have an amusing little anecdote from the mine," Derek said. "Anyone interested?"

"I am!" Molly said.

"So this guy goes 'round the corner to take a leak," Derek said, pointing at Rod, "and to mess with him, we all hid in a little crevice and turned all the lights off. This guy thought he was lost and ran around in circles screaming for a half hour!"

Sally and Molly laughed. Rod and Derek were extremely uncomfortable; they were starting to think Stanley had caught-on to what actually happened somehow.

"What is your problem, Stanley?" Sally asked him.

"I got the mail today," Stanley said.

"Don't tell me," Derek said. "You didn't get a parcel on your birthday? I hate it when that happens!"

"No, I got something," Stanley said. "I got more than I bargained for. Do you want to know what I got?"

"I'm thinking no," Derek said.

"Yeah," Rod said, shaking his head.

"What is going on here?" Sally asked.

Stanley pulled something out of his pocket, unfolded it, and showed it to Derek. It was his wanted poster.

"Who is that guy?" Derek asked, sweating. "He's a good looking guy, but I don't know who he is."

"It's you, Mr. Rhodes," Stanley said. "You're an outlaw."

"Dad, it's not what you think," Rod said.

Stanley stood up and pulled out a gun.

"Stanley, no!" sally yelled, clutching Molly.

Derek and Rod sprung out of their seats. Stanley turned to Rod and pointed the gun at him.

"Stanley, don't!" Sally yelled, crying.

"You lied to us, Rodney," Stanley said. "You didn't work on a mine. You joined an outlaw and committed crimes."

"The real crime is the governor thinking he can rob us blind and push us into poverty, pa," Rod said, calmly. "They're the outlaws."

"Did you kill anyone?" Stanley asked. "Did you kill any lawmen?"

"What would you have done if a lawman tried to kill you?" Rod asked.

Stanley shot the ceiling and Sally screamed.

"Yes, I did!" Rod yelled.

"Well, you don't belong with good people like us," Stanley said. "You're free to go be scum as long as you never come back here."

"Hey!" Derek yelled, enraged. "Don't talk to him like that! That kid risked his life to save you and your farm. Who cares if he had to break some laws? More power to him for standing up to the injustice of the governor and sheriff!"

"They keep this state together!" Stanley yelled.

"They destroy whoever they can to stay in power!" Derek yelled at Stanley. "They don't care about you or your family or anyone else! I can't decide if you're too blind or too stupid to know this!"

Stanley shot the ceiling again.

"Rod," Stanley said, "I don't allow criminals in my house. Leave, and never come back."

"I saved you, pa," Rod said.

"At what cost?" Stanley asked. "Get out."

"Don't go, Rod," Sally said, weakly.

"Shut up!" Stanley shouted. "Leave, Rod."

"Fine," Rod said.

"You're an ungrateful grouch with something up his ass," Derek said to Stanley. "You also don't know what the governor and sheriff are really doing, which blows my mind."

Stanley shot a bullet that whizzed right by Derek's ear.

"I'm gonna assume that you missed me on purpose," Derek said.

"Maybe I'm near-sighted, too, and the doctor didn't pick up on it," Stanley said.

"Wait, Rod," Sally said, handing him his hat before he left.

"I think that'll do, buddy," Derek said.

Rod and Derek left the house.

"You got your guns?" Derek asked.

"Always," Rod said.

Stanley went back toward his seat, but almost tripped over Sunny.

"See what I'm saying?" Stanley said, kicking the dog out of his way. "We have two bad people in the house and the dog does nothing."

"Maybe they're not bad," Sally said. She got up and angrily stormed out of the kitchen.

Molly sat there and just played with her food with tears in her eyes.

"You're not going to tell them about Rod, are you?" Molly asked Stanley.

"Why wouldn't you want me to do that?" Stanley asked her.

"Because I don't want them to hurt Rod," Molly said.

"Rod got himself into this," Stanley said. "He deserves some hurtin'."

"He's still my brother," Molly said, getting up and leaving.

"You know, Rod," Derek said as he and Rod sat down at the spot and looked at the night sky where Rod always took Molly to see the sunset, "we're a lot alike, you and me."

"How so?" Rod asked. "Did your dad kick you out?"

"Do you want to know what happened between me and my dad?" Derek asked. "Because I'm about to tell you."

Rod just realized Derek might tell Rod his life story and he'd be the only one to know it.

"Here goes, kid," Derek said, sitting back on the hill. "My pa was kind of like yours, but a lot worse. He was a struggling farmer with a lazy, ungrateful wife and 3 boys to take care of. Only one gave him any help, but it didn't make him treat me any different from my brothers."

"You had brothers?" Rod asked.

Derek hesitated.

"I barely remember anything about 'em," Derek confessed. "One day, my ma decided to leave my pa because she didn't think he was good enough. My two brothers left with her, but I stayed. My pa treated me a lot worse."

"Because you stayed to help him?" Rod asked.

"He had something else going on in his attic," Derek said. "Anyway, I hated farm life. I couldn't stand having to do the same stuff every single day for all hours of the day. One day, my pa decided I was nothing more than an inconvenience. He walked into the barn while I was in there with a big machete and locked the door behind him. He said to me 'boy, you're a waste of skin and I've had it.' He gave me this."

Derek traced the pattern of his scar with his finger. That's how he got it.

"But, I made him reconsider," Derek said. "That was the last time he ever abused me; the last time he ever did anything. So, there I was a lonely boy with only ten years of experience with nowhere to go in 1855. While I was wandering the countryside, about to starve to death, who shows up to save my life but Chief Alo. Back then he was General Alo. He got his Apache tribe to agree to let me stay with them. Well, there was one Apache boy my age that was furious I was there."

"Pacquio?" Rod asked.

"Pacquio, exactly. Didn't try to embarrass him or make myself out to be better than him. It's just all that Indian stuff came natural to me. I was able to spearfish and catch bigger fish than him; I could bring down bigger buffalo and bison than him. I was a better wrestler than him. I made better arrowheads than him, and I ran faster than him. I wasn't trying to make him look bad, but he never forgave me.

"I spent about five years with them until I decided that I was ready to go on my own again. The Apache taught me to survive on my own good enough, so I spent a year alone. Then, the Civil War broke out and both armies were looking for bodies. I gave the slip to both sides multiple times. I didn't want to be a part of that. Heck, I didn't care for either side.

"One year into the war, I met Tom. Tom and I became best friends and decided to join Bolton Butler's gang. At the time, they were the best gang out there. Well, he was like the governor in how he ran his gang. He treated everybody like crap. Tom and I could only take about five years of that. We left, and found Otis on a farm in one of the territories along the Mason-Dixon. We busted him out and he joined us. Tex was next, and then Villegas, Surge, Marcus and we started to grow. Every once in a while we'd go over to 'Maim Street' to take a break. That's where I met Jess. She was something else, I tell ya. But, when we got too serious, I worried about having something that could be used against me. I didn't want my enemies to use her as leverage to get me. I didn't want her to go through that, so I broke it off in a way that no one would mistake me for being a softy."

"You should probably tell her that before she decides to beat the hell out of you," Rod suggested. "And I think she can."

"No doubt she can," Derek agreed. "That's why I got so down in the dumps when Butler got hold of you. I felt bad that someone was suffering in my place. It didn't seem fair."

"Don't worry about me," Rod said.

"Well, it didn't take long for us to become the most wanted outlaws," Derek said. "All the other outlaws wanted to be better than us, all the girls wanted us, all the sheriffs wanted to arrest us, and the governor wanted to kill us. There you have it, you know more about me than Tom."

"How far back does he know?" Rod asked.

"He doesn't know anything about my family or the Indians," Derek asked. "You may do whatever you like with my story."

"You trusted me," Rod said. "I'm going to honor that."

"Tell you what," Derek said, "when I die, write that all down and sell it. I guarantee you'll make a bundle."

Tom and the rest of the gang emerged from the forest.

"What's the plan now?" Tom asked.

"Well," Derek said, "Rod and I are a little exhausted. We should take a vacation."

"Where?" Villegas asked.

"I'm so glad you asked, amigo," Derek said, "because we need an in to go to Mexico."

"You guys are going to love Mexico," Villegas said, excitedly. "The law enforcement are twice as incompetent as up Ralph's men, you can get away with anything!"

"Why don't you bring Beverly?" Derek asked. "I think it'll get her female feelings all twisted-up in knots when her outlaw boyfriend takes her on a trip with the gang."

"Meet me at the bar," Rod said, getting up.

"Go get 'em, foxy dog guy," Tex said, slapping Rod on the shoulder.

Rod rode to the governor's mansion and secretly climbed up to Beverly's room window. She was in there, lying bored in her bed. Rod tapped on the window and got her attention.

"Hi," she whispered, opening the window.

"My pa found out that I was in Derek's and he didn't like it," Rod said. "We're all going down to Mexico for some fun. Do you want to come?"

"Hell yeah I want to come," Beverly said, climbing through the window and shutting it.

Rod brought her down and they rode to the bar to meet with the rest of the gang.

"Okay, we're all here," Derek said. "Let's ride."

The gang rode off, unfortunately not realizing that Ralph himself and some deputies had staked-out the bar.

"We're taking a trip to Mexico," Ralph said, "to crash their fiesta."

Dictator Batista

Ralph and a small band of deputies were tight on their trail the whole way down to Mexico. Derek had never seen Villegas so happy; Villegas was returning to his home with actual strength and numbers. When he was younger, he didn't have any resources to fight back against the oppression. It was a totally different story now.

"So, what do we need to know about this place?" Tom asked Villegas.

"Can't you just be surprised?" Derek asked Tom as they rode.

"I don't like surprises," Tom said.

"Yeah, I remember that birthday party where Surge had to recessitate you after you fainted," Derek said.

"That wasn't fun for the both of us, Tom," Surge said.

"Nobody talk to anyone," Villegas said. "I'll take care of that. At marketplaces, we don't pay set prices, you negotiate. Be warned, sometimes they end in knife-fights. Don't be a stickler."

"Tom," Otis called out. Everybody laughed, even Tom.

"Derek, I think there got people that can play the guitar faster than you," Villegas said.

"We'll see about that," Derek said.

"I don't think anyone in Mexico has him beat," Beverly said to Rod.

"If someone can, Derek will just get on a piano," Rod said.

The gang knew they had a government to deal with when they spotted the border between Texas and Mexico. There was a huge wall built by the Mexicans with guard towers so sharpshooters could monitor their citizens who were trying to escape and Americans that might come in.

"Could you imagine if we tried something that stupid?" Derek remarked, looking at it.

"With the dictators, it's one horrible idea after another," Villegas said.

"I think I could knock it down if I got a running start," Tex said.

"You probably could," Villegas said.

"Wait, look at this," Surge said, pointing at a guard tower.

The guards in that particular tower were falling asleep while they were on duty.

"We've got the dead of night on our side," Derek said, looking up at the dark sky. "We've sleepy Mexicans. There's a big old opening in the wall right by that creek. We couldn't ask for a better opportunity."

"I agree," Tom said. "Just no galloping."

The gang all got on their horses and quietly trotted toward the gap in the wall.

"Seriously," Derek said, laughing at the wall. "Who are they kidding with this thing?"

Once they got through the gap, then they had their horses bolt into the Mexican mainland.

"Now, there may be some banditos lurking around," Villegas said. "Keep your eyes open."

A shotgun blast almost took his hat off. The gang was sandwiched between two halves of a band of banditos.

"What is with those ridiculous hats?" Derek shouted, pulling his gun out.

"They're sombreros!" Villegas yelled.

Rod brought his horse into a forest when it turned into a dogfight between the two horse-riding gangs. Beverly hid in a tree and Rod went to join the fight.

Rod rode toward a bandito that was reloading his rifle and hit him with every shot he took.

Unfortunately for the banditos, Derek's gang had American-made weapons and their weapons were poorly manufactured and were constantly misfiring. Derek's gang easily came out on top and the less than half a dozen banditos that survived fled the scene.

"Guest used to that all the time," Villegas said.

"We are used to that," Marcus said.

"I mean all the time," Villegas said. "Much more than in America. The normal people, not just the criminals get into it in the streets."

"Did he just ay Mexico is always like this?" Beverly asked as Rod went to get her down from the tree.

"Did you notice how crappy their guns are?" Rod asked. "We'll be just fine."

"Oh, you guys are gonna want to pay attention to this," Villegas said, looking down the meadow at the rising sunrise sky.

"How many have ever seen a Mexican sunrise en la tierra debajo del ciero con colores brilliants?"

"If you're gonna start speaking in code like that, I'm out of here," Derek said.

"It's the Spanish language, Derek," Tom said. "You know, it may behoove us to try and pick up on it a little bit while we're here because you don't want to make deals by mistake with these people by smiling and nodding like an idiot."

"Yeah, that happens all the time, I'm sure," Otis said, sarcastically.

"You'd be surprised," Villegas said. "Usually the Americans that come in here get themselves into all sorts of complexities by smiling and nodding."

The dictator of Mexico, Carlos Batista, was easily a lot worse than Nolan Roth was in Wyoming. Derek had a lot of trouble believing that, but the logistics of being the dictator or an entire country with an official standing military gave Batista the ability to be much worse than Nolan.

Nolan only had small pockets of inconsistent state militias the sheriff's department. The developing infrastructure also put a damper on his control, but Batista had it all working and everybody hurting. Derek did agree that the situation in Mexico was a lot worse than in Wyoming. There were a lot more poor people, but they had no will to do anything to voice their displeasure. The poor in Wyoming still had their anger to use and display. The Mexican poor gave up on theirs.

It was a little more depressing for the Mexican poor than it was for the Wyoming poor. In Wyoming, they did have steady work and paychecks to boot. In Mexico, a lot of them were failed craftsmen with huge economic uncertainty. Batista was even more cold and heartless. Nolan at least created government projects that attracted workers. Batista did nothing. He had a true aristocracy behind him, not like Nolan's wealthy men that were at the mercy of their businesses. Batista's rich were hereditary and stayed rich for life. And while Nolan had normal men working for the sheriff, Batista had professionally-trained soldiers, killers. Not law enforcement officers; people who killed.

When Ralph rushed to tell Nolan of Derek's plans to go to Mexico before he caught up with him, Nolan thought this was his chance to get some kind of alliance with a leader that he hoped to be.

Nolan wished he ran his state like Batista ran his country. Nolan also liked the idea of a hereditary, cultural aristocracy as opposed to business leaders on shaky ground. He had this change of heart after what happened to his brother and realized that things change. And Nolan loved being in the company of "better" people. Batista seemed like one of those people.

Nolan instructed Ralph to strike-up a deal with Batista because Derek had a Mexican national, Villegas, with him. Ralph was on his way to do that.

Batista didn't have any mansion or office. He had a straight-up castle. It was more like a palace than a castle. It had that eastern flair as opposed to the drab of a European castle. There was actually someone in the world who flaunted their wealth more than Nolan. It was Batista.

Ralph learned a lot about security immediately upon arriving at Batista's headquarters. Ralph knew that his deputies weren't perfect and screwed-up a lot. Ralph contributed that to the training not being tough enough. Batista's guards obviously had no problem with that. Tex would have had an even match with one of them.

"Who are you?" one of them asked Ralph.

"I'm Sheriff Ralph Hatcher from Wyoming," Ralph said, showing his badge. "These are my deputies."

"Did Governor Roth send you?" the guard asked.

"He did."

"You may enter," the guard said. "You two, take them to Rey Batista."

"What's Rey?" a deputy asked.

"King," one of the accompanying guards translated.

"The governor would like that, wouldn't he?" a deputy asked.

"Nolan's working on that," Ralph said. "But he'd like emperor much better."

The guards brought Ralph and the deputies into Batista's military planning room. He was there with his generals.

"Lord Batista," one of the guards said, "Sheriff Ralph Hatcher of Wyoming is here to see you."

Carlos Batista was wearing a red suit and a blue cape. The cape was silk. Batista looked like a very straight-laced guy; he had perfect posture and stood tall all the time. He had thick, angry eyebrows and very short, shaved, black hair.

"Ralph Hatcher," Batista said, walking up to him, "good to have you."

"Really?" Ralph asked, shaking Batista's hand.

"Claro que si," Batista said. "Absolutely. I like what Nolan is doing up there. He could use a little work, but he's got the right idea. La idea correcto."

"You're using a hint of accent from mainland Spain, are you not?" a deputy asked, trying to impress Batista and the generals. The generals chuckled.

"Yes," Batista said. "I am a mainland Hispanic. This Mexican rash on our language must be eradicated. They need to learn to adopt the superior Spanish cultures."

"It's like this," Ralph said to Batista, "Nolan can't stand the cowboys and hicks in Wyoming."

"We're going to be fine allies," Batista said.

"That's why we're here," Ralph said. "Nolan's most-wanted outlaw has traveled here. We desperately need to put him behind bars. By the way, he has a Mexican in his ranks."

"His name is not Villegas, is it?" Batista asked.

"It is," Ralph said.

"When I worked on the police force here," Batista said, "I always had to deal with that street rat. That's all he ever amounted to."

"Maybe we could help each other out," Ralph said. "We'll let you have Villegas if you help us catch Derek."

"Deal," Batista said, shaking his hand. "Ask me personally for anything you need. I think I also got a good idea to lure him into a trap."

Derek and the gang had brought more business to Mexico City than any of the people there had seen in their entire lives. They had all taken their excess loot to Mexico, and it was a lot. Especially since the currency they had was worth a lot more than the Mexican currency.

Rod bought Beverly a lot of Mexican jewelry such as the dream-catcher earrings, the colorful bandanas, dresses and scarves. He also bought a few gifts for Molly; he wasn't giving up on his family. Derek bought himself a bunch of obnoxious belt buckles; there was one of crossed revolvers, one of a bald eagle, one of a cougar, one in the shape of a boot spur, and one with the Texas longhorn symbol. Tom and Tex all spent their money on gifts for their families.

Villegas helped everyone drive the prices they had to pay down. Not too low, though, they did want to help these people out a little bit.

Somehow, Ralph and the deputies were able to stay hidden in the big crowds in Mexico City. Ralph spotted Rod and Beverly together in the marketplace and saw her wearing Rod's hat. Ralph couldn't believe it at first when he saw them kiss, but he figured out why Beverly wasn't around the governor's mansion so much of late. Ralph couldn't wait to see Nolan react to that news.

The second day in Mexico City, there was a big Mexican cultural celebration festival. Derek and the guys, and the girl, attended it. There were fireworks, confetti, piñatas, and a guitar-battle between Derek and a local musician. It was a tie.

As Batista disapproved by the native Mexican culture, he had the military storm the festival and break it up. Derek and his gang were the only ones who didn't flee in fear.

"Mr. Rhodes?" a soldier asked Derek, approaching him.

Derek looked at Villegas. Villegas nodded.

"Yes," Derek said. "Who wants to know?"

"Someone who wants to see America divided," the soldier said.

"What do you think, Tom?" Derek asked.

"A divided America would be easy to rob from," Tom said. "Governor Roth couldn't call in the Marshalls or national guard on us again."

"Who do we talk to in order to achieve this weaker America?" Derek asked.

"Follow us," the soldier ordered.

Villegas brought the brim of his hat down over his face. The soldiers brought them to the palace-like headquarters.

"Sir," the soldier said, bringing them into Batista's military planning room, "the outlaw is here."

"Ah," Batista said, turning to them. "Derek Rhodes and his famous gang."

"Are we famous here?" Derek asked. "Because in our hometowns we're pretty infamous."

"Depending on who you ask," Tom added.

"Let me tell you something," Batista said to them, going up to a map of Mexico and the United States on a wall. "I and my countrymen feel cheated out of lands that once belonged to us. We don't blame the Americans, or even Texans for these offenses. We blame your government. Do you gentlemen support your government?"

Tex spat on the ground and everyone shook their heads.

"As I suspected," Batista said. "Together, I think we could help weaken America so you men would have an easier time being outlaws and I can take my country's land back."

"I like where this is going," Derek said, nodding.

"Let's take this day to get acquainted with each other and tomorrow we can start planning," Batista said. "Have any of you ever had Mexican food?"

"I have!" Tex said.

"You're from Texas?" Batista inferred.

"Yep," Tex said. "More into being an outlaw, though."

"Fabulous," Batista said.

Batista saw Villegas standing in a corner, facing away from everyone.

"Yes, Villegas, I see you," Batista said.

Otis smacked Villegas' arm.

"No," Villegas said. He turned around and took his hat off.

"Oh, hey, Carlos," Villegas said. "It's been a long time since you dragged my family out of our home and spread us as far away from each other as you damn-well could."

"I'm trying to make up for that now," Batista said.

"Vendejo," Villegas muttered.

"He's just kidding," Derek said. "Was that bad, what he said? If it's bad, he's kidding."

"That was real good, Derek," Tom said.

They spent the rest of the day in Batista's headquarters utilizing the palace-part of it. They all ate, except for Villegas and Tex, Mexican food for the first time.

At night, just before Batista was going to have them taken to their rooms, Derek saw a guard light a beacon on fire in front of a window.

"Hey, this is pretty good," Derek said, getting up and walking over to it.

"Uh… It's not polite in this country to look out a man's window when you're his guest," Batista said, nervously.

"Look out the window, Derek," Villegas said, just to piss Batista off.

Derek looked out the window and saw that the beacon was a signal for some people to ride toward the headquarters. The signal was for Ralph, who was always unmistakable to Derek.

Derek turned around and Batista had his revolver out on him.

"You set us up," Derek said.

"Nolan's reward is going to make me even richer than I already am," Batista said. "Maybe I'll build a separate prison for Americans that trespass on my land."

Tex knocked the gun out of his hand and punched him in the face. Villegas leapt at Batista and palmed him in the throat.

"Good, we have a hostage," Derek said.

Two guards burst into the room and Surge and Otis attacked them. Derek burst through the window and tossed the Mexican guard into the beacon.

"Use Batista to get the hell out!" Derek ordered the gang. "Rod, Beverly, come on out here!"

Tex had dazed Batista in a full-nelson and Villegas had a gun shoved painfully into Batista's cheek. Villegas was scaring everybody because he was so wild at Batista. Batista destroyed Villegas' whole family, and he thought he was going to lose his mind at being around him.

Rod and Beverly went out onto the roof with Derek.

"Rod, I want you to experience something that I do on occasion," Derek said. "I want you to share this with me because I trusted you with my life's story. Bev, you're going to want to grab onto him."

Beverly stood behind Rod and wrapped her arms around him.

"What are we doing on the roof, Derek?" Rod asked, nervously.

"You have to trust me," Derek said, grabbing a shoulder of Rod's jacket. "Run with me."

"What?!" Rod yelled.

Derek ran toward the edge of the roof, dragging Rod behind him. Rod decided he was going to go off the roof one way or another, so he decided to go off with force.

Derek, Rod and Beverly leapt off the roof. Rod could see their horses a little ways ahead. They fell until they landed on the cloth roof of a stand outside the headquarters. That propelled them toward their horses, which they safely landed on.

"That was the most exciting thing I've ever done," Rod said, catching his breath and feeling exhilarated.

"Beverly, how did you enjoy that?" Derek asked.

"We need to go back and get my stomach," she said.

The doors to the palace opened and the gang walked out with Batista still a good hostage. They were circled by soldiers and Ralph with his deputies

"If you follow us, we're going to kill him," Otis threatened them.

They got on their horses and Villegas tied Batista's hands to his horse. They slowly trotted to the city gates.

"Open up or Batista will have una cabeza rompido," Villegas shouted, sticking the barrel of his revolver into Batista's mouth again.

The gatekeepers opened the gates and they slowly made their way out.

"No funny business!" Tex shouted back.

"Okay, do it now," Derek whispered to Villegas.

"Ride!" Villegas shouted, breaking the awkward silence.

Villegas shot Batista through the throat, probably hitting vital parts. Batista died, and the gang rode away.

Back in Wyoming, Nolan was becoming desperate. He had just gotten his statement from the state treasury, and he was in serious debt. That's because he was spending so much money to stop outlaws that ended up taking the money. Derek was bringing his government to the brink of bankruptcy.

"Sir," a deputy said, walking into his office. "There's someone here to see you."

"If it's not Ralph or someone with Derek Rhodes' head, they can fuck themselves," Nolan said, tearing-up the records.

"It's someone who can get you Rhodes' head," the deputy said.

Pacquio stepped into Nolan's office.

"Hmmmm," Nolan said. "Against my better judgment, I'll try anything at this point."

Derek's Secret

"How do you feel?" Derek asked Villegas as they rode into "Maim Street."

"I feel good," Villegas said. "I feel real good. Estoy muy alegre!"

"Did you just call me something?" Derek asked. "Because I wouldn't appreciate it."

"I didn't call you anything," Villegas said.

Billy approached them to take care of their horses for them.

"Hey, Billy!" Derek yelled, getting off his horse. "I brought you back a little something from Mexico."

Derek gave him the belt buckle in the shape of the boot spur.

"Thanks, Derek," Billy said. "Why didn't you tell any of us you were going to Mexico? Why don't I ever get to ride with you?"

"Billy, you pay attention to what Jess teaches you so you can be the smartest whipper-snapper in the West and make a lot of money," Derek instructed.

"That's the best advice I've ever heard him give, Billy," Jess said, standing in the doorway of the bar. "To not be like him."

"It's good to see you, too," Derek said.

"Derek, why don't you tell her what you told me about why you really left her," Rod suggested.

"That's a good idea," Derek said.

Derek walked over to Jess.

"Could we have a chat, pretty please?" Derek asked.

"No," Jess said.

"Pretty, pretty, pretty, pretty please?" Derek asked, folding his hands like he was begging.

"You're gonna want to hear this, Jess," Rod told her.

"I'll listen to him because I like your hat, Rod," Jess said.

Derek and Jess went up to Jess' room.

"I remember some stuff from in here," Derek aid, grinning and looking around her room. "Tell me what you remember. Let's see what we both remember."

"Probably different stuff, because you had other girls up here besides me while we were together," Jess snapped.

"Let me explain why I did the things that you're convinced are just sick."

"Oh yeah, spin it positively, Derek," Jess said. "You're supposed to be good at that."

"You see," Derek said, trying to think of the right way to say it, "it's like this. Aren't there people you know that you don't want to see get hurt because of them?"

"Yes," Jess said. "Billy, for one."

"Yeah, Billy's a good example," Derek said. "Let's use him. If it was the only way you could protect him, wouldn't you remove your connection to him? Wouldn't you try to make yourself distant enough from him so that no one could use him against you?"

"It would be hard, Derek," Jess said. "But I guess someone as heartless as you has no problem with that."

Derek grabbed Jess' hands.

"Butler had Rod kidnapped, and I went nuts that Rod was being tortured because of me," Derek said.

"You deserved to feel that," Jess said.

"Damn it, I'm trying to talk here!" Derek shouted at her.

"I'm sorry," Jess said, totally surprised that Derek raised his voice at her.

"Around the time we were about to get married, I started to feel the heat from Nolan and Ralph. I knew that Nolan wanted to find someone to use against me. I thought it would be you."

"Neither of them know I'm alive, Derek," Jess said.

"I didn't care," Derek said. "I couldn't put you in the position to have your life threatened in exchange for mine. I had to protect you from that."

"You know," Jess said, "if you had just told me this instead of running off **with your little whores**, I would have understood."

"You know who encouraged me to tell you this?" Derek asked. "Young Rod. He's a hell of a kid."

"I think you're both doing good for each other, Derek," Jess said, starting to cry a little bit.

Outside, Rod went up to Tom.

"Hey, Rod," Tom said. "I've been meaning to tell you, I think Bev would have enjoyed coming here. I don't think you should have dropped her off at home."

"One of these guys would have torn her up," Rod said. "Tom, Derek told me everything."

"Everything?" Tom asked.

"Everything," Rod said.

"Okay," Tom said. "I figured that was gonna happen. Good thing you came to me first. Everyone might pressure you for it."

"I want to do Derek a favor by keeping it secret," Rod said.

"Then do it," Tom said. "I won't tell anyone you know."

An Apache warrior ran into the city.

"Whoa, savage!" someone yelled.

Everyone but Derek's men aimed their guns at the Apache.

"He's okay," Tom yelled. "Put your guns down."

The Apache dropped to one knee and caught his breath.

"Someone go get Derek," Tom said, walking up to the Apache.

Tex ran into the bar to go fetch Derek.

"What is it, friend?" Tom asked the Apache.

"Pacquio sent us a message," the Apache said, still out of breath. "He's caught the sheriff. Pacquio's waiting to deliver him to you as a hostage."

"Derek!" Tom yelled with a big smile on his face. "You're going to want to hear this!"

"What?" Derek asked, running out. "I almost had Jess' emotions so wild that she was going to have sex with me!"

"That's not why I told you to tell her, Derek," Rod said.

"Oh, hey," Derek said to the Indian. "What are you doing here?"

"Pacquio has the sheriff hostage," the Apache said. "He's going to give him to you."

"Guys, we're heading out!" Derek yelled, running over to his horse.

"You know how people argue that there is a God? This is the kind of thing that makes me believe!" Tom yelled.

"Praise the lord!" Otis agreed.

"Someone get this man a horse!" Derek shouted, pointing at the Apache. "He's showing us the way!"

Billy brought the Apache a horse.

"Can I come?" Billy asked Derek.

"No, you can't," Derek said. "Go get Jess something to wipe her eyes with."

"But it's just a hostage," Billy argued. "What could go wrong?"

"It'll be boring," Derek said. "Let's ride!"

The Apache went first and everyone followed him. The Apache led them to a small town where Pacquio was standing in the town's center with Ralph next to him.

"Pacquio, if you can understand this, I love you!" Derek yelled, getting off his horse. "I want to give you a big fat kiss!"

"So cowboys are queer, too?" Ralph asked.

"How does it feel to be a prisoner, you pile of shit?" Derek asked Ralph. "Very ironic turn of events, ain't it?"

"Speak for yourself," Ralph said, pulling out a gun and pointing it at Derek. Pacquio gave Derek a smile.

"Pacquio, no!!" Derek yelled, stopping in his tracks.

Deputies swarmed out from everywhere and had the gang caught completely off guard and captured.

"Drop your guns," Ralph said.

All of Derek's men dropped their guns.

"Finally, I win," Ralph said to Derek.

In the capitol, Nolan slowly walked down the row of cells, letting the barrel of one of Derek's guns ring as it banged against the bars of the various cells. There were a lot of middle fingers being shoved through the bars at Ralph and Nolan.

Nolan stopped dead and turned to Derek's cell when he got to it. The rest of the gang was split in half and stuffed into the cells on each side of Derek's. Derek got his own, special cell.

"Well, well, well," Nolan said, looking at Derek. "Good work, sheriff."

"It was the Apache's work, to be honest," Ralph said.

"What's the matter, Derek," Nolan asked, noticing Derek's lifeless, sad expression. Derek had never felt that way before. He had never felt defeated, and it was getting to him.

"Life and the law caught up with you, didn't it?" Nolan asked. "It turns out that the great, folk-hero Derek Rhodes is not invincible! Sorry to break it to you, boys! Perhaps you should have teamed-up with the governor, because that is truly invincible!"

Tex stood up and knocked on the bars to get Nolan's attention.

"What do you have to say, fat boy?" Nolan asked.

Tex stuck his hand through the bars and flicked Nolan right above the eyebrow. It hurt Nolan a lot.

"Ow, shit!" Nolan yelled, dropping Derek's gun and hopping around, holding his forehead. Everyone but Derek laughed.

Tex sat down and gave Tom a high-five.

"Bunch of morons," Nolan said, regaining his composure.

"We outsmarted you for the longest time," Tom said. "You might as well give us our due credit."

"I'll give all of you your due hanging," Nolan barked. "I've got nooses with all of your names on them. We're going to hang you all together, too."

"But you'll be so bored with nothing to do without us," Tom said. "Be honest, wasn't it great fun going head-to-head with us?"

Everyone nodded in agreement.

"I suppose it was," Nolan said. "But I can be at pace knowing I was the better brother."

"What the hell?" Surge asked. "I thought your brother lost everything years ago."

"That's one of them," Nolan said. "But now, I have both of them beaten."

"Who is your other brother?" Tom asked. "We all only knew the one."

"Everybody only knows the one," Nolan said. "Ralph, do you know what I'm talking about?"

"I haven't the slightest idea," Ralph said.

"That was pretty much his grip of things when he was after us," Otis joked.

Everyone but Derek cracked up.

"You think that's funny, do you?" Nolan asked, chuckling. "That's great."

Nolan knelt down in front of Derek's cell. Derek was staring at the ground the whole time.

"Maybe you shouldn't have stayed with pop," Nolan said to Ralph. "You should have stayed with us."

"No," Tom said in disbelief. "No way in hell!"

"There you have it!" Nolan yelled, standing up. "Your fearless leader is his enemy's brother!"

"Derek, he's lying, right?" Villegas asked.

"This can't be true, Derek," Marcus said.

"Why don't you tell them, Mr. Roth," Nolan said to Derek.

"Nolan and the bankrupt Roth you all heard about were my brothers," Derek explained. "My family was poor, and my pa just couldn't get ahead on his farm. My mother gave up on him and took my two brothers, Nolan and the other, to go try and find a richer man to live with. I stayed behind with my dad. They grew up with money and power. I grew up with nothing, and had to turn to crime to stay afloat."

"The funniest part, to me," Nolan said, laughing, "is that even when you picked your own last name, you still had the same initials! D. R.!"

Ralph and Nolan threw their heads back and laughed.

"I'm sure it was fun while it lasted," Nolan said to Derek, "but now it's time to suffer the consequences."

Nolan and Ralph left the jail.

"Did you guys rehearse that?" Tom asked Derek. "Because I didn't buy it."

"It's all true, Tom," Derek said. "Every bit of it."

"I always thought they looked a little similar," Otis said. "With the black hair."

On the way back to the governor's mansion and sheriff's station, Ralph stopped Nolan.

"I have more interesting news," Ralph said. "Even though that was unbelievable."

"Believe it," Nolan said.

"Here I go," Ralph said. "Beverly has been missing lately because she's seeing someone."

"Who is she seeing?" Nolan asked.

"The McGillis boy," Ralph said.

"Huh," Nolan said. "I'm gonna kill her."

Nolan stormed toward the governor's mansion. He went straight up to her room and found her to be long gone.

Ralph went into the station to find Glenn dusting off the desk of a deputy.

"You missed a spot," a deputy said, sprinkling some crumbs from his cornbread on the table. Glenn dusted it off. The deputy sprinkled some more crumbs.

Ralph went over to Glenn, wrapped his hand around his throat and pushed him into a wall.

"Guess what," Ralph said. "We've got your poor-shit friend locked up with the rest of the Rhodes gang. We're going to hang them tomorrow. Feel free to let his family get a spot right up front."

Ralph let go of Glenn and was about to leave, but turned around and punched Glenn in the face while he was still getting his wind back.

That night, everybody couldn't sleep in the jail.

"Derek, you don't have to be ashamed that you're his brother," Tom insisted. "I give you credit for making the choices you did."

"I got us all killed," Derek said. "You guys trusted me, and look what's happened. I failed everybody."

"You listen to me, my good friend," Tom said. "I'm not giving up on you or anybody else here. We've been through too much together to let ourselves get defeated. No sir, we will get out of this."

"What's that?" Marcus asked, pointing at a window. It was glowing orange.

"I think that's fire," Villegas muttered. Everyone snapped to attention.

The sounds of Apache war-cries and shouting deputies rang out from outside the jail.

"I think Alo sensed Pacquio's treachery!" Tom yelled.

The door to the hall of holding cells opened up and Glenn ran in with Alo.

"Glenn!" Rod yelled.

Everyone was standing up except for Derek.

"I've had enough of this shit," Glenn said, unlocking the cell. "Screw the sheriff."

"There he is!" Rod yelled.

Glenn released all the prisoners.

"We're escaping, Derek," Tom shouted. "Get up!"

"Come, my son," Alo said, pulling Derek up and pushing him out of the jail.

They all got out of the jail to see the Apaches and deputies fighting.

"Retreat!" Alo yelled.

All the Apaches left the capitol and the gang got on their horses and rode out of the city. They were freed, but Derek was still depressed.

Back in the governor's mansion, Nolan and Ralph were having drinks with Pacquio.

"I can't believe that happened," Nolan said. "Ralph, an Indian tribe freed a gang of cowboys from execution. Keep a lookout for flying pigs."

"I have something else we could use," Pacquio said. "Derek has a woman that he cares for greatly. Her name is Jess and she lives in 'Maim Street'."

"It's our last chance," Nolan said. "Ralph, you go to the McGillis farm and see if Beverly is hiding there. Pacquio and myself will get this Jess woman from 'Maim Street' and meet me back here. We'll get Derek to make a mistake if someone he cares about is on the line."

Nolan's Resignation

The next morning, someone was pounding on the McGillis' door.

"Who could that be?" Sally asked herself, going over to it and opening it up.

Beverly ran by her and looked for Molly.

"Hi, Bev!" Molly called from the kitchen table.

Beverly ran over to Molly and hugged her.

"Hello…." Sally said, walking up to Beverly.

Sunny also ran up to Beverly and put his paws on her lap.

"Oh, I'm sorry," Beverly said, catching her breath. "I'm Rod's girlfriend, Beverly Roth."

"Beverly… Roth?" Sally asked, shaking her hand. "You're the governor's niece?"

"**What**?!" Stanley shouted, making everybody jump. He stormed into the kitchen.

"Rod kidnapped the governor's niece?"

"No," Beverly said. "I wanted anything to get me away from my uncle. He's a horrible person."

"Do you need a more reliable source, Stan?" Sally asked. "Are you convinced that the governor is a bad man now?"

"Tell me, Beverly," Stanley asked. "When you were with Rod, was he doing his outlaw thing?"

"Mr. McGillis, Beverly began.

"Call him Stan, honey," Sally said. "And call me Sally."

"Stanley," Beverly said, "being an outlaw is the only choice my uncle is giving anyone anymore."

"You hear that, Stanley?" Sally asked. "Rod's only choice to save us was to be an outlaw. Can you appreciate that?"

"Is my brother alright?" Molly asked Beverly.

"I don't know," Beverly said. "The last time I saw him was when he dropped me off after we all came back from Mexico…"

"Mexico, ah!" Sally exclaimed. "See, outlaws get to do whatever they want and go to Mexico! Was it nice, Beverly?"

"It was spectacular," she said. "But, I think I might be in a lot of danger."

"You can hide here as long as you want," Stanley said. "Go up into our room. We've got ourselves a pretty big closet."

"Thank you," Beverly said, getting up and running up the stairs.

"Yeah, Rod wanted to keep her a secret from you in case you overreacted," Molly explained.

"How proud are you of our son?" Sally asked Stanley. "He's saving farms, saving your life, saving our lives, dating politician's daughters, vacationing to Mexico. I think he's amazing."

There was a pound on the door.

"Open the fuck up," Ralph shouted. "Sheriff's department."

Stanley went over to the door and opened it up.

"The whole world can't wait for you, cripple," Ralph snapped at Stanley as he let himself in with ten deputies.

"Excuse me?" Sally yelled, furious at what Ralph said to Stanley.

"Read the Constitution or Bill of Rights much?" Stanley asked Ralph.

"You two, down there," Ralph ordered two deputies, pointing down the hall.

"Does the governor just sit up in his office thinking of how many Constitutional laws he can break day after day?" Stanley asked.

"Where is the governor's niece?" Ralph asked Stanley. "We know she's here. Don't bullshit me."

"There's a little girl here!" Sally shouted.

Ralph walked over to the kitchen table and pointed his revolver in Molly's face. Molly sat back in her chair and closed her eyes.

"No!" Sally yelled, trying to grab the gun from Ralph. Ralph put his hand over her face and shoved her down.

"You don't point a gun at my daughter and then attack my wife in my house," Stanley said, making his way over to Ralph. One of the deputies kicked his crutch out of his hands and another deputy pushed him over. They all laughed at him. Sally was on the ground, crying.

"Stop!" Beverly yelled, appearing on the stairs. "Really, Ralph? You're threatening little girls?"

"We were actually hoping to threaten you," Ralph said. "Okay, guys, we just need to wait for Nolan to get back with Rhodes' girl. We're out."

The deputies left the house and Ralph was dragging Beverly out by her hair. Sunny, growling, started to trot toward Ralph. Ralph got violent in pulling Beverly's hair, so Sunny started barking and sprinting. Sunny leapt off the porch and sunk his teeth into Ralph's neck and brought him down.

"What-" Ralph shouted, stunned.

Ralph rolled over and tried to push Sunny away. Sunny was going at his face hard. He deputies had to kick him away and they helped Ralph up. They resumed in going back to the capitol.

Stanley started to push himself up, and Sally and Molly went over to help him.

"No," Stanley said, stopping them. "Let me do this."

Sally hugged Molly and kissed her on the head.

"Are you okay, baby?" Sally asked.

"I'm fine," Molly said.

Stanley got himself up on one foot.

"Molly, get your father's crutch for him," Sally said.

"Forget the crutch," Staley said. "Rod did all that to save the farm and house, so I'll stand on two feet for him."

Stanley put the foot connected to his broken leg down and was able to stand tall.

Nolan, Pacquio and more deputies made it to "Main Street." They didn't waste any time.

"We need a Miss Jess to come out and surrender herself or else this shithole will burn to the ground!" Nolan yelled. "That should have happened a long time ago but it doesn't have to if a Jess gives herself up!"

There was no sign of any life. Nolan looked over and saw a small boy hiding in the stables.

"Bring me the rodent over there," Nolan told one of the deputies.

The deputy walked over to the stables and dragged Billy over to Nolan.

"I'm going to kill this kid here if Jess doesn't come out!" Nolan yelled, pointing his gun at Billy's head.

"Don't do it, Jess!" Billy shouted.

"I swear to God!" Nolan said, clicking the hammer back. The deputy that was holding Billy there took Billy's hat off.

"You're going to kill him, Jess!" Nolan yelled.

Jess stepped out of the bar.

"Is that her?" Nolan asked Pacquio. Pacquio nodded.

"You saved the kid, Jess," Nolan said, putting his gun away.

The deputy punched Billy in the face and pushed him away hard enough to knock him over. Jess ran over to Billy and hugged him.

"Are you okay?" Jess asked Billy. Billy nodded.

"Good," Jess said. "Give me a kiss, you tough guy."

Billy kissed Jess on the cheek.

"For God's sake," Nolan said. "Bring her to me."

Two deputies grabbed Jess and brought her right up to Nolan.

"So," Nolan said, "you're Jess. Pacquio told us all about you and Derek. What a shame that he took off, right?"

"I was fine before I met him," Jess said, "and I'll be fine after this."

"That's all up to Derek," Nolan said.

The gang decided to hide with Alo's tribe, minus Pacquio. Everyone was fired-up from the rescue, except for Derek. Derek wanted to go through his whole life never being caught by Nolan. That was ruined.

"Cheer up, Derek," Tom said, going up to Derek while the rest of the cowboys and Indians were dancing and partying.

"I failed," Derek said. "I will have always failed."

"Pop?" Glenn asked as a white man ran into the camp. All the Apaches aimed spears and arrows at him.

"He's a friend, right?" Tom asked.

"He was sheriff before us," Rod said.

"Bad news, guys," Glenn's father said. "Ralph has Beverly and Nolan just kidnapped Jess from 'Maim Street'. They're going to torture them."

"That's bad," Tom said. "We can't let them get away with this."

"My people will help," Alo said. "We Apache do not approve of the strong taking advantage of the weak for their own gain."

"Derek," Tom said, walking over to him, "Nolan has found Jess. I assume you're coming with us to rescue her."

Derek slowly shook his head.

"I'll fail again."

Tom smacked Derek in the face. Derek had no reaction.

"If you're going to sit here and sulk, fine," Tom said. "You're about to destroy any chance you ever had of getting back with Jess and I think you're going to start losing the respect of your gang. You've lost mine."

"Glenn, I'm sorry I made you work at the sheriff's department," Glenn's father said to him. "You should have told me the stuff that was going on there."

"I tried," Glenn said.

"Oh, Rod," Glenn's father said. "Ralph and his deputies may have physically abused your father because they found Beverly at your farm."

"They hurt my dad?" Rod asked.

"One of the deputies was boasting about knocking his crutch out from under him."

"So," Nolan said, pacing back and forth in front of a chair that Beverly was tied to in his office, "you are involved with an outlaw boy?'

Nolan had Ralph, Pacquio and a few deputies behind him for his fear tactic on Beverly. It was working.

"You're wrong about them, Uncle Nolan," Beverly said, crying. "They're not bad men!"

Nolan smacked her in the face.

"I am aware of that," Nolan said, getting right in her face. "But, guess what, I need to make sure that people don't know the truth about them. Otherwise, I'm the bad guy. And you and I can't share in all this wealth that I get. You like the wealth, right?"

"It doesn't seem fair when so many people are suffering," Beverly said.

"It's their own damn fault," Nolan said.

"You're a monster, Uncle Nolan," Beverly said. Nolan smacked her again.

A man with black hair like Nolan's ran into the room, chased by two deputies. His skin and clothes were dirty with mud and dirt like he'd been sleeping in squalor for a long time. It was Beverly's father.

"Damn it, Nolan!" he yelled as the two deputies got him. "Don't treat my daughter like this!"

"How did he get passed the two of you?" Nolan asked the deputies. "Ralph?"

Ralph pulled his gun out and killed the two deputies. Beverly started sobbing.

"You were saying something," Nolan said to his other brother.

"Beverly told us everything, Nolan," the brother said. "I'm taking her back."

"Hold it," Nolan said. "I take Beverly in out of the goodness of my soul and you have the nerve to criticize me on how I do things? That's out of line."

"May we teach him a lesson?" Ralph asked.

"Beat the living shit out of him," Nolan said. "Make him appreciate what I've been through taking care of his spoiled-damn brat!"

Ralph snapped and two deputies wrestled Beverly's father into another room to rough him up.

"That was pretty sick," Ralph said to Nolan.

"I know," Nolan said.

"I like it."

"I thought you might."

"Governor, the US attorney general is here to see you," a deputy said, bringing the attorney general into Nolan's office.

"Oh, tell me Washington is finally waking up to the fact that I need some damn help here against the violent Indian tribes, loony worker unions and outlaw gangs that I've been dealing with," Nolan said to the attorney general.

"Tell me that you're going to start adhering to the Constitution and federal law so I don't have to have the secret service forcibly remove you from office so we can get some democracy in Wyoming for a change," the attorney general said.

"You've got the secret service with you?" Nolan asked.

"They're right outside, ready to arrest the real criminals and bring them into federal court for trial," the attorney general explained.

"Okay," Nolan said. "Well, I don't feel like going to federal court, I don't even believe in trial hearings, and most of all, I don't like to be criticized. So, this is happening, now."

Nolan opened up the window and got the deputies' attention.

"Fellas!" Nolan yelled. "Kill the secret service agents!"

The deputies immediately obliged and slaughtered the secret service agents that were accompanying the attorney general.

"This is anarchy," the attorney general exclaimed.

"Perhaps if you think we're part of the Union, it might be," Nolan said. "But I'm keeping Wyoming for myself. It's my country, and it's a dictatorship. Didn't count on me doing that did you? Take him the fuck away and keep him hostage. Let's see if we can get the US government to cover our losses that Derek Rhodes caused."

Two of Ralph's men tossed the attorney general into another room.

"Where is the Jess woman?" Nolan asked a deputy.

"Follow me," the deputy said.

"I'm not done with you," Nolan said, pointing at Beverly on his way out.

The deputy brought Nolan into the room where they had Jess tied to a chair.

"She's a feisty bitch," a deputy said, leaving the room. He had what looked like claw-marks on his face.

"I'll watch myself," Nolan said.

Nolan went into the room and shut the door behind this. He opened up the conversation by chuckling.

"I didn't believe it the first time I heard it," Nolan said. "Derek never struck me as the kind of guy who would even think to settle down with one woman. Luckily, he proved me right."

Jess was silent.

"I don't know how you kept yourself a secret from me for so long," Nolan said. "I like to be in the loop of everything going on. That way, I can strike at everyone I don't like where it really hurts."

Nolan grabbed Jess by her hair and pulled her head back.

"Listen to me carefully," Nolan said. "I don't want anything to happen to you. It's Derek I'm after. If you cooperate with the men like a good little woman should, you'll walk out of here fine. Heck, I might even get you a position as Sheriff Hatcher's sex slave. He'd like one of those."

Jess spat in Nolan's face.

"Oh, dear," Nolan said, taking out a handkerchief and wiping the spit away. "That wasn't a smart thing to do."

Nolan back-handed her in the face.

"I have changed my mind," Nolan said, about to walk out of the room. "I'm going to kill even when I catch Derek. You and my stupid niece."

Nolan slammed the door behind him as he left.

The gang and the Apaches spread out around the forest that surrounded the capitol. The deputies were all stationed to fend off an attack. Nolan was standing there with a gun to Jess' head and Ralph, with his scarred face from Sunny, had a gun to Beverly's head.

"We know you're out there, Derek," Nolan shouted.

Rod looked at Tom. Tom shook his head with a furious look on his face.

"Come out," he said. "It would be a shame for Jess and Beverly to die when it was supposed to be you! I don't think even your sick mind could deal with that guilt! So why don't you come out and we can have a good-old showdown like the story-books?"

Jess looked over at Beverly. She looked too scared to do anything. Jess slipped a small knife from up her sleeve and into her hand.

"Come on, Derek!" Nolan said. "This is no way to treat a brother!"

Jess stabbed Nolan through the wrist of the hand he was holding his gun. Nolan screamed and dropped his gun. Before Ralph could do anything, Jess threw the knife and it went into his wrist. Ralph dropped his gun.

Jess ran over to Beverly and grabbed her hand. Just before the deputies shot them, the Apaches started to fire arrows upon them. Nolan ran into the governor's mansion.

Once the Apaches were out of arrows, they and the gang charged into the capitol. Rod ran over to where Jess and Beverly were hiding in the forest.

"Nice shot, Jess," Rod said.

"Nice hat," Jess replied.

"Keep it safe for now," Rod said, putting it on her head.

Rod pulled out a revolver and joined the fight.

For the most part, it was a city-wide gun-fight with people hiding behind stuff and firing out. The Apaches were a little more active, but they were still using their projectiles.

However, in the center of the city, Pacquio and Alo were walking toward each other to fight. They weren't flinching or anything at the bullets that were constantly flying right by their heads.

"You followed the wrong path, Pacquio," Alo said, tossing his staff aside.

"I'm my own tribe now, Alo," Pacquio said, pulling a tomahawk out of his loin cloth.

"I don't want to do this, Pacquio," Alo said.

Pacquio walked toward Alo, twirling his tomahawk around.

"Alright, so be it," Alo said.

Pacquio swung at Alo's neck. Alo pulled his head back and dodged it. Pacquio raised the tomahawk back over his head and swung down at Alo's head. Alo stepped out of the way and palmed Pacquio hard in the ribs.

Pacquio hurled the tomahawk at Alo's head and missed. Pacquio charged at Alo and started throwing a barrage of wild punches. Alo avoided every single one of them.

Pacquio wound-up for a haymaker and put all of his strength into it. He missed. Pacquio bent his arm behind his back and held it there.

"Stop this," Alo demanded. He shoved Pacquio away.

Pacquio grabbed him by the throat with both hands and kicked a foot out from under him. Pacquio threw Alo onto the ground and tried to strangle him. Alo head-butted Pacquio and kicked him back.

Pacquio got low and drove himself into Alo. Wise turned on his heel and tossed Pacquio through the air. A deputy had stood up from behind where he was hiding and Pacquio was in his line of fire. The deputy put five rounds into Pacquio. Alo took a throwing-knife out and killed the deputy.

Alo went over to Pacquio and rolled him over so he was face-up. He had bullet-holes all over his body.

"I'm sorry, Pacquio," Alo said. "I didn't mean to get you killed."

"You freed me," Pacquio said. "I thank you for that."

Pacquio's head dropped and he fell down to the ground and his eyes shut.

Rod was pinned-down behind a barrel for a long time. Once it sounded like the barrel wasn't being shot at anymore, Rod leaned out and saw Ralph rushing toward him. Rod fired at his head and took his hat off. Ralph almost fell over in surprise. Rod tried to fire again, but he was out of bullets.

"Damn!" Rod yelled, feeling through his pockets to see if he had any more bullets left.

Ralph grabbed him by the shirt and threw him against the wall. Ralph tried to put his gun right in front of Rod's face but Rod knocked the gun out of his hand. Ralph punched Rod in the face and then threw him aside by his hair. Rod tried to get up but Ralph stomped on his back and Rod slammed face-first into the porch.

Ralph pulled Rod up by the back of his shirt and threw him face-first into the wall. Ralph spun Rod around and punched him in the face. Rod was a little dazed and slumped down to the floor. Ralph pulled out a big knife and raised it above his head to kill Rod. Bullet hit the blade and sent it flying out of Ralph's hand.

"Derek!" Tom yelled.

Rod looked passed Ralph and saw Derek was standing there with a smoking gun, and a totally different attitude.

"Let the kid go, Ralph," Derek said. "It's me you want."

"Are you just gonna shoot me?" Ralph asked, turning around. "Like a chicken shit?"

Derek put his gun away and showed his empty hands.

"Man to man, Ralph," Derek said. "Like always."

Ralph stepped down to the ground. Ralph pulled out a second knife and Derek had one to match it.

Ralph was the aggressor in the knife fight. Like Pacquio vs. Alo, Ralph was the one going at Derek with a lot of foolish force and anger. Derek was like Alo in being patient and under control so Ralph would make the mistakes and get himself tired.

But, Ralph seemed to have endurance. He was able to maintain the same level of intensity in attacking Derek. Derek was the one who started to lose wind.

Ralph was able to get a good slash on Derek's arm and Derek dropped his knife. Ralph kneed him in the face and Derek fell over. He tried to get up, but Ralph kicked him on the side and Derek flipped over and fell back down.

Rod ran to go get Ralph's gun. He came back and Derek was just lying on the ground, waiting for Ralph to plunge his raised knife into him. A loud gunshot rang out and blood splattered out of Ralph's throat, but it wasn't Rod who fired. Ralph's dropped the knife and slowly dropped to his knees. Derek got up and helped Ralph's body fall over. Derek stood up and spat on it.

Rod looked over and saw Stanley was there with a smoking gun, no crutch and both feet comfortably on the ground.

"Pa!" Rod yelled.

Stanley walked up to Derek.

"Did I ever thank you for helping my son?" Stanley asked Derek.

"I knew you would, eventually," Derek said, shaking his hand.

Rod ran over to them.

"Son, I'm glad you made those decisions," Stanley said. "I didn't realize how hard they were."

"Don't sweat it, pa," Rod said. "Let's go kill this governor."

"I'll lead the way," Derek said, pulling out his dual-revolvers.

Derek, Rod and Stanley all ran toward the governor's mansion.

"Pa, where's your crutch?" Rod asked.

"I don't need it anymore," Stanley said. "And remind me to tell you about that great guard dog, Sunny.

Derek ran into the governor's mansion and shot-up six guards that were supposed to keep them out.

"Whew!" Derek yelled, blowing the smoke away from the barrels. "This way."

Derek led them both upstairs and up to Nolan's office. They saw Nolan sitting in his chair behind his desk and Nolan shot at them. No one seemed to be hurt. They all walked in and pointed their guns at Nolan.

"It's the end of the line, governor," Derek said.

"I suppose you're probably right," Nolan said. "You gotta hand it to me, though."

"Yeah, you managed to screw things up more than anyone could speculate was possible," Stanley said.

"No governor had seen a bigger rise in outlaws than you," Rod said.

"I'd like to see any of you try it out," Nolan said.

"There are a lot of people who would like to see me try," Derek said. "But, I've got to tell you one thing."

"What?" Nolan asked.

"You're pretty good on the quick-draw for a politician," Derek said, looking down at his chest and putting a hand over his heart. He removed his hand and it was covered in blood.

"Derek," Rod said.

Derek dropped his gun and fell to his knees. Stanley kept his gun on Nolan while Rod tended to Derek.

"Tell Jess that I really did care about her," Derek asked

"I will," Rod said.

"Remember what I told you, Rod," Derek said. "I want you to… to ride for….. Just ride…."

Derek shut his eyes and died.

"You just killed Wyoming's most popular guy," Stanley said. "Good luck getting reelected."

"Consider this my resignation from office," Nolan said standing up.

"Easy with that gun," Stanley said, clicking his hammer back.

Nolan put his gun to his own head and killed himself, causing blood, guts and a few chunks of his brain to burst of the other side of his head. His body didn't take it's time falling down and dramatizing its death. Nolan went right down.

"Just like that, then," Stanley said, putting his gun away.

Tom, Tex, Villegas, Otis, Surge, Marcus and Alo ran into the governor's office to see what happened.

"Oh... no," Tom said, with his nose starting to get stuffed-up. "This can't.... No...."

Tex patted Tom on the shoulder.

"Did we get the governor?" Jess asked, running in. When she saw Derek's body, she stopped short in her tracks and her eyes started to water up. She grabbed Rod's shoulder with one hand and put her hand over her mouth with her other hand.

"Is he really....?" She asked, sobbing.

"Yeah," Stanley said.

"If everyone is emotionally together enough," Otis said, "could someone tell me how this went down?"

"We walked in here and Nolan fired at us," Stanley said. "No one seemed to be hurt. Derek held it together for a while, but he was the one who took the bullet."

Jess hugged Rod and cried all over him.

"Then, we let Nolan kill himself," Stanley said.

"Well," Tom said, "at least we don't have it on us that we killed the governor."

"We took him down, though," Rod said, consoling Jess.

"We sure did," Villegas said. "Derek would want us to hold our heads high for that."

"Sure thing," Tom said. "Sure thing."

Tom knelt down beside Derek's dead body.

"I always knew if he went down, he'd go down fighting," he said to everybody. "He was a real fighter. Down to the end, he was. Let's make sure he's remembered that way, fellas."

Everyone nodded.

They figured that Derek wouldn't have wanted to be buried. He couldn't even sit in the same chair for more than a couple of drinks. They decided to have Alo perform a ritual cremation of Derek and then they'd sprinkle his ashes into a river. There was a big turnout of Apaches from different tribes that showed up to pay their respects for Derek. The total attendees there were the Apaches, the whole gang, Jess, Billy, everyone from "Maim Street," the whole McGillis family, Tom's wife and daughter, Tex's family, the Wilson family and Sunny.

They all knew that Derek was a good sport, so they had a dual-ceremony to cremate Pacquio as well. They were going to scatter Pacquio's ashes throughout the camp, though. They weren't going to mix his ashes with Derek's.

The only people that actually cried were Jess, Molly and Sally. In the brief time they met Derek, Molly and Sally were won-over by his charm, outlaw or not. Derek had the ability to do that, although it was tougher with men. Stanley didn't buy his whole act at first, obviously.

Tex was playing a slow, sad blues tune with Derek's guitar during the burning while Alo played a sad song on an Indian wind instrument.

The man that was the most notably upset was Tom. On the surface and the job, Tom appeared to be very annoyed by Derek all the time. But, everyone, even Derek and Tom, knew that it was all in good fun. Derek and Tom were best friends. There was no doubt in anyone's mind about it, not even when Tom was pestering Derek about whichever topic Tom chose to criticize him for. It would take something a lot worse than that to get Derek upset with Tom. Heck, Derek didn't even get bitter at Pacquio for always trying to pick fights with him.

Derek's other brother was pretty upset, too. He wasn't like Nolan; he didn't really want to abandon his father and Derek, but he didn't have the mental strength that Derek had to deal with hardship. He and Derek were actually close before he left.

The attorney general, who they graciously rescued, put their minds at ease by offering to lobby for their complete amnesty for any crimes they have committed against the state of Wyoming.

Derek had done so much for Rod and the entire McGillis family, even a lot of it being unintentional. But, he did the most for Rod and it was all out of the distorted goodness of his heart. So, Rod thought it was reasonable that he kept his promise to Derek on his deathbed, and he thought it was fair that his whole family took part in it.

They picked a good day with a clear blue sky with no clouds in the way and found a vast, wide-open field that stretched on for miles. They brought Sunny along, too. Stanley was treating him almost as well as he treated Molly before he truly warmed up to Rod. It was when Sunny took the sheriff down when he came around.

"Why don't we call him 'killer' from now on?" Stanley asked, letting Sunny get up on his hind legs and lean on Stanley's horse.

"I just hope he never has to do anything like that again," Sally said, sitting behind Stanley on his horse.

Stanley looked over to Rod, who had Molly sitting in front of him and Beverly sitting behind him.

"I would have never thought to do something like this," Stanley said to Rod. "Derek seems like he knows how to make everything fun."

"Once we're positive your leg is actually better I'll get you jumping off of buildings onto your horse," Rod said. "Wasn't that fun, Bev?"

"I'm never doing that again," she said, smacking his shoulder. "And you were scared, too."

Rod looked in front of him to the gang of which Tom was now the leader.

"Are you sure you don't want to ride with us, kid?" Tom asked him. "You were a great addition to our gang. We'll miss you."

"I appreciate it, Tom," Rod said, "and I'll miss you guys. But I've got this life to live."

"If that life ever gets threatened," Tom said, "you can always come to us. There will always be a spot for you."

"I'll hold you to that," Rod said. "Although, I don't know how much longer you'll need to be outlaws with Alo as governor."

"Could anyone have imagined that happening a year ago?" Sally asked.

"If anyone would have predicted that an Apache leader would be governor of an American state, they'd be the village idiot," Tex agreed with her.

"Well, we'll be off now," Tom said, giving Rod a firm handshake.

"I'm never going to forget everything we all went through, Tom," Rod promised.

"That's all we can ask," Tom said. "Let's ride, boys!"

"Good luck, Rod!" Otis yelled as they rode away.

Rod felt a tear roll down his cheek as the gang rode away. He didn't know if he'd ever see them again, and he knew he wanted to.

"After you, pop," Rod said to Stanley.

"You know something," Stanley said, "you have proven yourself to be more the man of the house than me. After you."

Rod got his horse galloping and Stanley galloped after him. It turned out that riding for no reason was just as exhilarating and liberating as Derek promised it to be. Rod was just glad to have his family back together, a group of friends that he would never forget, he was glad that he helped Glenn to take charge of his own life, and he was glad to have Beverly. Rod had ridden the western tide and survived with more than he went in with, and more than he thought he'd return with.

Made in the USA
Charleston, SC
12 June 2011